The Bags of Tricks Affair

The Bags of Tricks Affair

A CARPENTER AND QUINCANNON MYSTERY

BILL PRONZINI

A TOM DOHERTY ASSOCIATES BOOK  NEW YORK

THE BAGS OF TRICKS AFFAIR

Copyright © 2018 by Pronzini-Muller Family Trust

A Forge Book
Published by Tom Doherty Associates
175 Fifth Avenue
New York, NY 10010

www.tor-forge.com

Forge® is a registered trademark of Macmillan Publishing Group, LLC.

The Library of Congress Cataloging-in-Publication Data is available upon request.

ISBN 978-0-7653-9435-4 (hardcover)
ISBN 978-0-7653-9436-1 (ebook)

Our books may be purchased in bulk for promotional, educational, or business use. Please contact your local bookseller or the Macmillan Corporate and Premium Sales Department at 1-800-221-7945, extension 5442, or by email at MacmillanSpecialMarkets@macmillan.com.

First Edition: March 2018

Printed in the United States of America

0 9 8 7 6 5 4 3 2 1

For Marcia, naturally

The Bags of Tricks Affair

1

QUINCANNON

Behind the long, brass-trimmed bar in McFinn's Gold Nugget Saloon and Gaming Parlor, Quincannon drew two more draughts from the lager spigot, sliced off the heads with the wooden paddle, and slid the glasses down the bar's polished surface. The Cornish hardrock miner who caught them flipped him a two-bit piece in return.

"Keep the nickel change for yourself, lad."

Quincannon scowled as he rang up the twenty-cent sale. Lad. Bah! And a whole nickel for himself, finally, after six hours of hard work in a noisy, rowdy atmosphere. He debated leaving it in the register, but his Scot's blood got the best of that; he pocketed the coin. The lot of a bartender was neither an easy nor a profitable one, a fact he hadn't fully realized until the past two days. Nor was it a proper undertaking for a man who no longer drank strong waters of any kind.

He cursed himself for a rattlepate. Adopting the guise of a

mixologist had been his blasted idea, not Amos McFinn's. Not that serving beer and hard liquor to Grass Valley's constant stream of Cornish miners known as Cousin Jacks and other denizens tempted him to resume his formerly bibulous ways, as the perfume of Golden State Brewery's steam beer had during his undercover work in the Plague of Thieves Affair the previous January. Having successfully resisted that temptation made resisting this one easy enough. No, it was the hard work combined with the penny-pinching ways of the Gold Nugget's customers, and the insults they hurled at him when he failed to serve them quickly enough, that made this undertaking difficult.

For the moment there were no more demanding drinkers at his station. Most of the miners and sports lining the mahogany were watching the square raised platform in the center of the cavernous room, where the two women faced each other across a green-baize-skirted poker table.

The play between the pair had been going on for nearly three hours now. At first the other gaming tables—poker, faro, roulette, chuck-a-luck, vingt-et-un—had had their usual heavy clutch of players. But the spectacle of the two lady gamblers engaged in a moderately high stakes stud-poker match was too enticing. The number of kibitzers around the platform, watching the flash of cards reflected in the huge overhead mirrors, had doubled when it became apparent that the challenger, the Saint Louis Rose, was a formidable mechanic in her own right. Now the crowd had swelled so large that some of the nearby tables had been shut down for the duration.

The fact that the two women were complete opposites

added to the appeal of their match. The house favorite, Blanche Gaunt Diamond, better known as Lady One-Eye, was ten years older, dark haired, dark complexioned; her dress was of black velvet and encased her big-boned body so totally that only her head and her long-fingered hands were revealed. The black velvet patch covering her blind eye gave her a faintly sinister aspect. She sat quiet and played quiet, seldom speaking, but she was nonetheless a fierce competitor who asked no quarter and granted none. The only times her steely one-eyed gaze left the cards was when she glanced at the two well-dressed gents who occupied a ringside table—her handsome gambler husband, John Diamond, who called himself Jack O'Diamonds, and her taciturn brother and financial manager, Jeffrey Gaunt.

The Saint Louis Rose cut a slimmer and far gaudier figure. Too gaudy by half, in Quincannon's judgment. She wore a fancy sateen dress of bright green, fashioned low across the bosom and high at the knee so that a great deal—a great deal, indeed—of creamy skin was exposed. A red wig done in ringlets, a little too much rouge and powder, false eyelashes the size of a daddy longlegs, and mouth painted the same rose color as the wig completed her image. She laughed often and too loud and was shamelessly flirtatious with the kibitzers. Even Jack O'Diamonds now and then let his gaze stray away from his wife—and from the sultry, flame-haired presence of Lily Dumont, whose faro bank was close by—to rest on the Rose's swelling bosom.

Quincannon was one of the few in the hall not paying attention to the game. As it had all evening, even while he was serving customers, his gaze roamed the packed room in search of odd or furtive behavior. No weapons were permitted inside the Gold Nugget, but few if any of the patrons would have stood still for enforced searches by McFinn's bouncers. Quincannon was willing to wager that there were at least a handful of hideout guns in the hall on any given night.

Movement at the edge of his vision turned his head. But it was only Amos McFinn once more slipping around behind the plank. He was a nervous little gent, McFinn, even at the best of times; on this night he hopped and twitched like a man doused with itching powder. Sweat gleamed on his bald dome. The ends of his brushy mustache curled around his down-turned mouth in the manner of pincers.

He drew Quincannon to the backbar and asked in a hoarse whisper, "Anything suspicious?" It was the fifth or sixth time he'd come to voice that or a similar question. He had spent most of the evening shuttling back and forth among the half-dozen bouncers spotted around the hall and Quincannon behind the bar.

"Only two small things, Mr. McFinn. Your actions being one of them."

"Eh? *My* actions?"

"Stopping by to bend my ear every half hour or so. Someone might wonder why the owner of this establishment is so interested in his new mixologist."

"No one is paying any attention to us."

"Not at the moment. At least not overtly."

"Well, I can't help worrying he may be here tonight," McFinn said. "Not that I expect he'll make an attempt in front of so many witnesses—"

"If an attempt is to be made. That isn't certain yet."

"No, but a packed room is an ideal place for one. Especially if the assassin is deranged enough not to fear for his own safety."

Quincannon said nothing to that, his gaze roaming again.

McFinn sighed. "All right, then, I'll leave you be." He started to do this and then stopped and once more leaned close. "Two small things, you said. What's the other?"

"Jack O'Diamonds."

"Eh?"

"Have you noticed his interest in Lily Dumont?"

"No. Lily Dumont?"

"They were thick at her table before the poker match began, while Lady One-Eye was in her dressing room."

"You mean you think they—?"

"More than likely."

"I don't believe it. Why, Jack is devoted to Lady One-Eye. I'd stake my reputation on it."

Then your reputation, Quincannon thought sardonically, is worth no more than a plugged nickel.

One of the reasons he'd chosen the guise of a bartender was that gaming-hall employees were far more likely to pass along private knowledge to a fellow drone than to a detective or even a customer. A bouncer and one of the other barmen had both confided that Lily and Jack O'Diamonds had spent time alone at her cottage on more than one occasion. They had also told him Lily's swain, a Nevada City saloon owner named Glen Bonnifield, knew about the affair and was in a rage over it. Quincannon had had proof of this; Bonnifield, a tall thin gent in a flowered vest, was in the crowd tonight, and the look in his eye as he watched Lily and Jack O'Diamonds earlier was little short of murderous.

Lily seemed not to care that she was being observed by Bonnifield, or by Lady One-Eye's gimlet-eyed brother. Several times she had pressed close to Diamond and whispered in his ear, and she did so again now, stepping over from her faro bank. From the look on the gambler's face, she had passed a comment of an intimate nature. He nodded and smiled at her—a rather lusty smile—and touched the three-carat diamond stickpin in his cravat, his trademark and good-luck charm. His wife didn't seem to notice; her single eye was on her cards. But Jeffrey Gaunt did, and it was plain from his curdled expression that he didn't like it. Neither did Bonnifield. His smoldering look kindled and flared; he took a step toward the pair, changed his mind when Lily returned to her table.

McFinn was saying, "Even if there is something between Jack and Lily, what does it have to do with the reasons—either of the reasons—I hired you?" He paused and then blinked. "Unless you think one of them—?"

"I don't think anything at this point," Quincannon said.

This was an evasion, but McFinn accepted it and let the matter drop. As he twitched away, a ripple passed through the crowd. Lady One-Eye had won another hand, this time with a spade flush over the Saint Louis Rose's high two pair. Someone within Quincannon's hearing said that it was the fifth pot in a row she'd taken. He glanced up at the ceiling mirrors. Early on, the pile of red-and-blue chips had been tall in front of the Rose; in the past hour it had begun to dwindle there, to grow on Lady One-Eye's side. One or two more large pots and she would have picked the Rose clean.

Lady One-Eye shuffled the cards for another deal, her long fingers manipulating them with practiced skill. According to the story she'd told McFinn, a buggy accident ten years ago had claimed her left eye and damaged her left hip so that she was unable to walk without the aid of her gold-knobbed cane. But she considered herself fortunate because her hands were her livelihood and both had come through the accident unscathed. Her handicaps, in fact, had won her sympathy and support among the sports who frequented gaming halls such as the Gold Nugget. Even hard-bitten professional gamblers, who considered it bad luck to play against a one-eyed man, had been known to sit at a poker table with Lady One-Eye. Only once, though, in most cases, for their luck with a one-eyed woman generally turned out to be just as bad.

Five-card stud was her game, the only game she would permit at her table. And the table here *was* hers: she rented it from McFinn, paying a premium because alone on the raised platform she was the Gold Nugget's central attraction. She had occupied the table for four weeks now, ever since she and her brother and her husband had arrived in Grass Valley at the end of May. Their previous whereabouts were unknown, though the fact that all spoke with a noticeable Southern accent tended to support McFinn's contention that they were originally from New Orleans.

Already word of Lady One-Eye's prowess and phenomenal luck had spread wide. She never refused a game, even for low stakes; and so far she had not lost a single high-stakes match, once relieving a Sacramento brewer of $1,100 on a single hand of stud. Some said she was a better mechanic than such sporting queens as Poker Alice, Madame Moustache, and Lurline Monte Verde. A few claimed she was the equal of Luke Short, even of Dick Clark.

At least one was afraid she might be a cheat to rival George Devol, the infamous Mississippi River skin-game artist. That lone skeptic was not a victim of her talents, fair or foul. He was the one person, other than the Lady, who had benefitted most from her presence in the Gold Nugget: Amos McFinn.

McFinn ran a clean establishment. He had to in order to remain in business. Grass Valley—and its close neighbor, Nevada City—were no longer the wide-open, hell-roaring mining camps they had once been. Now, less than four years from the new century, they were settled communities with schools, churches, and Civic Betterment Leagues. There was a move afoot to ban gambling in both towns. So far McFinn and the other gaming-parlor operators had managed to forestall the efforts of the bluenoses; but if it came out that a female tinhorn had been working the Gold Nugget with impunity for the past month, especially if she were caught cheating during one of her public performances, it might just give the anti-gambling faction enough ammunition to shut down McFinn's operation.

This was one reason why he had hired Carpenter and Quincannon, Professional Detective Services. Lady One-Eye had increased the number of his customers and thereby his profits; he couldn't afford to send her packing on a fearful hunch, without proof. He had to know for sure before he could act, and as quickly as possible given the other reason he'd sought detective help.

That reason was potentially even more disastrous. Five days before, an anonymous note written in green ink had been slipped under the door of the room Lady One-Eye shared with Jack O'Diamonds in a lodging house behind the Gold Nugget. She had found the note and taken it to McFinn, who in turn had brought it to Sheriff Hezekiah Thorpe. But there was little the law could do. The note might well have been the work of a crackpot, all blather and bunkum. On the other hand, it might be just what it seemed: a thinly veiled death threat.

Quincannon had examined the note in Thorpe's office shortly after the Nevada County Narrow Gauge Railroad, which linked Grass Valley with Colfax and there joined the Southern Pacific line, had deposited him in this mountain community. It read:

WARNING TO LADY ONE EYE
AND J DIAMOND

The good citizens of Grass Valley don't want your kind. We have got rid of bunko steerers, confidence sharks, sure thing men, thimble riggers and monte throwers and we will get rid of common card shaprs and there men too. Leave town in 48 hours or you will pay the price and pay dear when you least expect it. I mean what I say. I have fixed your kind befor, permement.

Crude language and spelling, and poor penmanship as well. It might have been written by a near-illiterate with a misguided moral streak; this was McFinn's assessment. But Quincannon wondered. It could also have been written by someone educated and clever, with a motive for wanting Lady One-Eye, Jack O'Diamonds, or both dead that had little or nothing to do with their professions. At any rate, they had ignored the warning and the forty-eight-hour period had passed without incident. If the note writer carried out his threat, particularly if he were to carry it out inside the Gold Nugget, McFinn would be ruined as effectively as if Lady One-Eye were exposed as a cheat—

"Three pretty little fives! The pot's mine, dearie!"

The Saint Louis Rose's loud, coarse voice echoed through the hall. Quincannon frowned and glanced up at the mirror above the poker table. The Rose was dragging in a small pile of red-and-blue chips, Lady One-Eye watching her stoically.

"Two in a row now and more to come," the Rose said to a knot of bearded Cornish miners on her left. "My luck is changing for fair, gents. It won't be long before all the red and blue are mine to fondle."

The miners sent up a small cheer of encouragement punctuated by ribald comments. Most of the onlookers, however, remained Lady One-Eye's champions. Like them, Quincannon wished the Rose would close her mouth and play her game in silence. Listening to her plume herself was an irritation and a distraction.

The deal was Lady One-Eye's. Without speaking she picked up the deck. Quincannon again studied her dexterous fingers as they manipulated the cards, set the deck out to be cut, then dealt one card facedown and one faceup to the Rose and herself. If she was a skin-game artist, he reflected, she was in a class by herself.

The professionals she'd cleaned during the course of her career would have caught her out if she had been doing anything as obvious as dealing seconds, dealing off the bottom, switching hole cards, or using a mirror or other reflective surface to reveal the faces of the cards to her as she dealt them. She could not literally have had anything up her sleeve, for the long sleeves on her high-collared dress fit tightly about her wrists. Nor could she have employed table bags or any of the other fancy contraptions manufactured by the likes of Will & Fink, the notorious San Francisco firm that specialized in supplying gimmicks to crooked gamblers. Because of the raised platform, and the fact that a woman played upon it, the table wore a floor-length green skirt; but the skirt was kept drawn up until Lady One-Eye took her chair and play began, thus allowing potential players to examine both it and the table if they chose to.

The Rose's up card was the jack of clubs, the Lady's the four of hearts. Both women peeked at their hole cards. The Rose then winked at her admirers, bet twenty dollars. Lady One-Eye called and dealt a ten of diamonds to go with the jack, a deuce of spades for herself. This time the Rose bet fifty dollars. Again, silently, Lady One-Eye called.

The fourth round of cards brought the Rose a spade jack, the Lady a five of diamonds. The challenger grinned at her high pair and said, "Jacks have never let me down," a remark that caused Lady One-Eye to cast a quick glance at her husband. "One hundred dollars on the pair of 'em, dearie."

Quincannon wondered if the remark about jacks had been deliberate—if the Rose, too, had noticed the intimacy between Jack O'Diamonds and Lily Dumont. Likely she had. Lady One-Eye was as aware of it as her brother, he was fairly certain of that.

Without another glance at her hole card, the Lady called the hundred-dollar bet. Slowly she dealt the fifth and final cards. Jack of hearts. And the trey of clubs. Three of a kind for the Rose, a possible open-ended straight for herself.

The onlookers began to stir and murmur. Play at the few other open gambling tables suspended for the moment. Nearly everyone in the cavernous room stood or sat watching the two women. Even McFinn, leaning against one of the roulette layouts, was temporarily motionless.

"Well, dearie," the Rose said, "three handsome jacks." She tapped her hole card. "Is this the fourth I have here? It may well be. What do you think, Lady, of my having the jack of diamonds?"

Quincannon was sure that this innuendo was intentional. But whatever Lady One-Eye thought of the remark, she neither reacted nor responded.

"Or it may be another ten. A full house beats a straight all to hell, dearie. If you even have a six or an ace to fill."

"Bet your jacks," Lady One-Eye said in her soft, cold drawl.

The Rose separated four blue chips from her small remaining stack, slid them into the pot. "Two hundred says it makes no difference if you have a straight or not."

"Your two hundred, and raise another two."

Voices created an excited buzz, ebbed again to silence.

Neither of the women seemed to notice. Their gazes were fixed on each other.

"A bluff, dearie?" the Rose said.

"Call or raise and you'll soon know."

"Four hundred is all I have left."

"Call or raise."

"Your two hundred, then, and my last two hundred."

"Call."

The pile of red-and-blue chips bulged between them. The crowd was expectantly still as the Rose shrugged and turned over her hole card.

The queen of hearts. No help.

"Three jacks," she said. "Beat 'em if you can."

Her one good eye as icy as any Quincannon had ever seen, the Lady flipped her hole card. And when it was revealed in the glistening mirrors, a triumphant shout went up from her champions.

Ace of clubs to fill the straight.

The pot and all of the Rose's table stakes were hers.

2

QUINCANNON

For the next half hour Quincannon was busy attending to the unquenchable thirst of the Gold Nugget's steady stream of customers. But not so busy that he was unable to maintain his observations.

The Saint Louis Rose, after fending off a pair of drunken sports who considered her fair game, slipped quietly out of the hall. Lady One-Eye gathered her winnings, turned the chips over to her taciturn brother to be cashed—all the while keeping watch on her husband. Jack O'Diamonds made no further move to Lily Dumont's faro bank, nor did he approach his wife. Instead he bellied up to the bar at Quincannon's station and called for a brandy.

The Nevada City saloonkeeper, Glen Bonnifield, took this opportunity to stalk to Lily's table, lean down with his face close to hers. Their conversation was brief and clearly heated. To end it Bonnifield slapped the table hard with his open hand—as a substitute for slapping Lily, Quincannon thought—and then swung away, back past the bar. His eyes met Diamond's in the mirror; the two gazes struck sparks, but neither man made a move toward the other. Bonnifield stalked to the front entrance and was gone.

Quincannon served Jack O'Diamonds his brandy. "Your wife had a fine run of luck tonight, Mr. Diamond."

"My wife's luck is always fine." The gambler didn't sound as pleased about it as he might have. Jealousy? Compared to Lady One-Eye's skill with the pasteboards, honest or not, his own was mediocre.

"And your luck with Lily Dumont? How has that been?"

The comment, delivered casually, produced a tight-lipped glower. "What do you mean by that?"

"No offense, sir. I was asking if you'd won or lost at faro."

"I didn't play faro tonight."

"Mr. Bonnifield seemed to think you did," Quincannon said blandly, "and that you spent a great deal of time at Lily's table. So did Mr. Gaunt."

"I don't care a tinker's damn what either of them thinks." Jack O'Diamonds fingered his flashy diamond stickpin, downed his brandy at a gulp. Then he, too, left the Gold Nugget—alone, and still without speaking to his wife.

Jeffrey Gaunt, clad in a rusty black frock coat, striped trousers, and string tie, sidled up to take his brother-in-law's place at the bar. He was a year or two younger than Lady One-Eye, clean shaven except for a thin shoelace mustache, his face and body as gaunt as his name, his black hair combed flat to his skull and glistening with pomade. His only distinguishing feature was a deep chin cleft the size of a thumbprint.

"What's your pleasure, Mr. Gaunt?" Quincannon asked.

"A glass of water." The man's Southern drawl was even more pronounced than those of his sister and Jack O'Diamonds.

"Just that?"

"Just that. I don't take strong spirits."

"Nor do I, sir. I only serve them."

"I noticed you talking to Jack O'Diamonds. What about? He seemed agitated."

"I asked if he'd won or lost at faro tonight. He said he hadn't played."

"And the question upset him?"

"No, sir. It was my mention of Lily's swain, Mr. Glen Bonnifield."

"What about Bonnifield?"

Quincannon set the glass of water on the bar in front of Gaunt. "He seemed to think Mr. Diamond has been spending a great deal of time at the faro bank."

"Did he now." The ice-blue eyes narrowed into a steady stare. "And what did you say to that?"

"Nothing, sir. It's none of my concern."

"That's right, it isn't. I'd remember that if I were you."

Gaunt drank his water, set the glass down sharply, and ambled off to join Lady One-Eye. Bad blood between him and his brother-in-law because of what was going on between Diamond and Lily Dumont? Quincannon wondered. Maybe so; the pair seldom spoke to each other in public. A potentially volatile situation, in any case, though whether or not it was relevant to the investigation remained to be seen.

Lady One-Eye, meanwhile, had stepped down off the platform, approached Lily Dumont, and engaged her in a brief, heated discussion just as Bonnifield had. Lily's reaction to whatever was said to her was to call the Lady an unladylike name, in a voice loud enough to cause a commotion among the miners seated at her bank. Lady One-Eye responded by making a warning gesture with her gold-knobbed cane before limping away. She then left the hall in the company of Gaunt and the bouncer assigned by McFinn as escort and bodyguard.

Quincannon decided he'd had enough of bartending for tonight if not for the rest of his life. He hung up his apron, donned his long coat and derby, helped himself to a cheroot from a vase on the bar, and went to pay Lily a visit of his own.

She was shuffling and cutting a full deck of cards for placement in her tiger-decorated faro box; the cards made angry snapping sounds in her slim fingers. She, too, was a complete opposite of Lady One-Eye. She had flaming red hair, a temper to match, and the hot sparking eyes of a gypsy. Fire to the Lady's ice.

"Trouble with Her Majesty?" Quincannon asked with mock sympathy.

"Her Majesty. Hah! I'll tell you what that female is." Which Lily proceeded to do in language that delighted some and shocked others among the miners seated at her table.

"A cold and jealous woman, all right," he agreed.

"Threaten me, will she? I'll fix her first. I'll rip out her other eye and turn her into Lady Blind."

"Why did she threaten you?"

"Never mind about that."

Quincannon bent toward her and said in a lowered voice, "I wonder how long she and Jack O'Diamonds have been together. They seem a mismatched pair."

"Too long. And 'mismatched' is putting it mildly. God knows what he ever saw in her even before she lost her eye."

"Poker winnings are more attractive to some than a pretty face."

"Well, that's why he stayed with her as long as he has. But maybe not for much longer."

"Oh? He wouldn't be planning to leave her, would he?"

"That's none of your business."

"Is it any of yours, Lily?"

"Miss Dumont to you. My business is mine, no one else's."

"Not even Glen Bonnifield's?"

"Leave the lady be, mister," one of the miners snapped. "Be gone with ye so she can deal her cards."

And take your hard-earned money, Quincannon thought. But he only shrugged and turned away.

As he made his way through the crowd toward the front entrance, he spied Amos McFinn hurrying to intercept him. He pretended not to see the nervous little client; he had no interest in answering another "Anything suspicious?" or similar question yet again. He managed to make good his escape before McFinn got close enough to ask it.

It was some past midnight now, and even though thick July heat blanketed the town during the day, snow still mantled the Sierras' higher peaks and the mountain air held a faint chill after nightfall. The continual beat of stamps at the massive Empire Mine southeast of town all but drowned out the throb of piano and banjo music from inside the Gold Nugget and other gaming halls and saloons nearby.

At this hour there was but a small amount of foot and vehicle traffic on the steep slope of East Main Street, its expanse more brightly lit now that electric lamps had replaced the old gas ones. A far cry from the boom years of Grass Valley and Nevada City following the 1851 discovery of gold in quartz ledges buried beneath the earth, when thousands of gold seekers, camp followers, and Cornish and Irish hardrock miners had clogged the streets day and night. Now the Empire was the only major mine still in operation, with shafts sunk as deep as seven thousand feet below the surface.

On Quincannon's first visit here, some eight years ago, the town had still retained some of its wide-open Gold Rush flavor. Now nearly all the rough edges had been buffed down and rounded off. This was fine if you were a law-abiding, churchgoing citizen with a family to raise and support. But tame places were not for John Frederick Quincannon. He would rather walk the mean streets of a hell-roaring gold camp or those of the Barbary Coast.

He paused on the boardwalk to light the cheroot he had appropriated. He seldom smoked cigars, preferring shag-cut loaded into his stubby briar pipe, but free tobacco, if it was of decent quality, had a greater satisfaction than the paid-for kind. Then, instead of heading to his lodging place, the Holbrooke Hotel, he walked down to the town's other main thoroughfare, Mill Street. The only lit building along there was the

Empire Livery Stable. He saw the night hostler working inside as he passed—and no one else after he turned uphill on Neal Street.

A building boom had taken place in Grass Valley since his last visit. Formerly the town had consisted of simple wood-frame structures common to boom camps, those used for commercial purposes bearing false fronts. Now there were two-story Italianate and Queen Anne–style homes and not a few front-gable cottages with facing verandas.

One of the Palace's bouncers had told him that Lily Dumont lived in a cottage on Pleasant Street, just off Neal. He found the address with no difficulty. The cottage was not one of the larger front-gable variety, but a small frame building of no more than three rooms, tucked well back from the street in the shade of a pair of live oaks. The neighborhood was a good one, and by the light of stars and a rind of moon he could tell that the cottage and its gardens were well set up. Much too well set up, he thought, for a woman who operated a faro bank to afford on her own. He wondered if Glen Bonnifield had an investment in the property as well as in the fair Lily.

The cottage's curtained windows were dark; so were those in the two nearest houses. He shed the remains of his cheroot and walked softly around to the rear. The back door was not locked. He entered, struck a match to orient himself and to show him the way into the front parlor.

An oil lamp with a red silk shade sat atop a writing desk. He lit the wick, turning the flame low, and by this light he searched the desk. There was one bottle of ink, but it was blue, not green. Nothing else in the desk held any interest for him.

He carried the lamp into Lily's bedroom, where he found further evidence of financial aid: satin dresses, a white fox capote, an expensive ostrich-feather chapeau. But that was all he found. If Lily had written the threatening note, she had either done it elsewhere or gotten rid of the bottle of ink she'd used.

Quincannon returned the lamp to the writing desk, snuffed the wick, then followed the flicker of another match to the rear door. He let himself out, shutting the door quietly behind him.

He was just turning onto the path toward the front when the first bullet sang close past his right ear.

He threw himself to the ground, an immediate reflex action that saved his life: the second bullet slashed air where his head had been, thudded into something behind him. The booming echo of the shots filled his ears. He reached under his coat for his Navy Colt, then remembered he hadn't worn it because of his bartending duties; instead he'd armed himself with the same type of double-barreled Remington derringer Sabina carried, an effective weapon at close quarters in a crowded room but with a range of no more than twenty feet. He rolled sideways, clawing the derringer free of his pocket, half expecting to feel the shock of a bullet.

But there were no more rounds fired. The thick branches of an oleander shrub ended his roll; cursing under his breath, he shoved away from the evergreen and then lay flat and still, the derringer held up in front of him. He peered through the darkness, listening.

A brief, faint sound that might have been retreating footsteps. Then silence.

He pushed onto his knees. Lamplight suddenly brightened one of the windows in the house next door; its outspill showed him that the yard and the street in front were now deserted. He got quickly to his feet, careful to keep his head turned aside from the light. A face peered out through the lamplit window and a voice hollered, "What in tarnation's going on out there?" Quincannon didn't answer. Staying in the shadows, he ran ahead and looked both ways along Pleasant Street.

His assailant had vanished.

"Hell, damn, and blast!" he muttered angrily to himself. He slid the derringer back into his pocket, hurried to Neal and around the corner before any of Lily's neighbors came out to investigate.

Grass Valley a tame place now, its streets safe at night? Bah! There was still plenty of hell left in this town. The question was, had this particular hell been directed at him or someone else?

The Holbrooke Hotel, a two-story brick edifice, was Grass Valley's oldest and finest hostelry. Presidents Grant, Harrison, Cleveland, and Garfield had purportedly stayed there during visits to California; so had Gentleman Jim Corbett. And so had the notorious Mother Lode highwayman, Black Bart—one fact that the management chose not to advertise. If any of the hotel's distinguished guests had ever wandered uphill to Texas Johnny's Golden Gate Brothel, a nearby attraction in the old boomtown days, this fact was also held in discreet confidence.

The dimly lit lobby was deserted when Quincannon entered. He climbed the staircase to the second floor, went around the corner past number 8, his room, and stopped before number 11 at the rear. Light showed in a thin strip beneath the door. He knocked softly. It was no more than five seconds before the latch clicked and the door opened.

He said, "Ah, the lovely Saint Louis Rose."

"Hello, dearie," Sabina said.

3

SABINA

She caught hold of his coat sleeve, tugged him inside, and quickly shut the door. She still wore her outlandish Saint Louis Rose costume, all except for the red wig which caused her head to itch, but she had scrubbed off the hideous rose-colored lip rouge and removed the false eyelashes. Her long black hair, uncoiled and combed out, drew and held John's admiring gaze. It was the first time he'd seen it that way, she realized, for she always wore it rolled and fastened with a jeweled comb at the agency and on their social outings.

"You're late, John. I expected you an hour ago."

"I've been to Lily Dumont's cottage."

"Have you now. For what purpose?"

"Not the one you're thinking. She's still dealing faro. And she has too many admirers already."

"Jack O'Diamonds as well as Glen Bonnifield. And I'll warrant Diamond is more than simply an admirer."

"My thought exactly."

"Lady One-Eye is also aware of it."

John nodded and fluffed his beard. Or attempted to, the habitual gesture being stayed somewhat by the fact that it was no longer as thick and bushy as a freebooter's; he had trimmed it for his role as a mixologist. Sabina rather preferred it this way. It had a softening effect on his features, made his dark eyes less fierce.

"Trouble there, do you think?" he asked.

"Of one kind or another. Lily Dumont is a dish to tempt any man, especially one with a block of ice for a wife."

"I prefer loud and bawdy redheads, myself." He gave her a broad wink. "Come over here, Rosie, and give us a kiss."

"I will not. Stand your distance."

"The Saint Louis Rose is no more likely than Lily Dumont to refuse a handsome, devoted gent a kiss. Or anything else he might want."

"Perhaps not. But Sabina Carpenter *is* and you know it."

"At least for the nonce."

"John . . ."

"I was only having a innocent bit of sport with you, my dear."

"Innocent, my eye."

John sighed and went to sit on one of the room's plush chairs. He gazed wistfully at his partner in Carpenter and Quincannon, Professional Detective Services. One thing you could say for his tastes, Sabina thought. He was far more attracted to a mature, well-bred woman with more than a dozen years of experience as a detective, half of those with the

Pinkerton Agency's Denver office, than he was to the likes of
Lady One-Eye and the Saint Louis Rose. Still . . .

"What did you mean by loud and bawdy?" she demanded.
"Do you think I overplayed my role tonight?"

"Well . . . perhaps a touch."

"I thought my performance was rather good."

"It's too bad Lotta Crabtree wasn't here to see it. She might
have offered you a new career as a stage actress."

"Don't make fun of me, John. I didn't strike a false note with
Lady One-Eye, I'm certain of that."

"You really enjoy playing the Rose, don't you?"

Yes, she did. It wasn't often that she was able to operate
undercover, and when she did it was usually in a rather commonplace role—that of a milliner in Silver City, Idaho, for
instance, when she'd been with the Pinkerton's Denver office
and had first met John. Portraying a character like the Rose
held a certain amount of girlish pleasure, in the same way
dressing up in costume had when she was a child growing up
in Chicago.

Her smile prompted him to say, "Even though the Lady did
succeed in plucking you like a chicken?"

"I wouldn't say I was plucked, exactly."

"How much did you lose? The entire fifteen hundred
McFinn provided?"

"Yes. Mostly on that last hand."

"A straight to your three jacks. Luck of the cards, or did she
manufacture her own luck?"

"Oh, I'm fairly sure she's a skin-game artist," Sabina said.
"One of the best I've seen or heard of."

"Were you able to spot her gaff?"

"I think so. But she's so proficient at it that it took me most of the night. I wouldn't have seen it at all if I hadn't spent those weeks with Jim Moon at the Oyster Ocean in Denver a few years ago, learning his bag of tricks. It boils down to manipulating the cards so she knows her opponent's hole card on at least half the hands she deals."

In gathering the cards for her deal, Sabina explained, Lady One-Eye dropped her own last hand on top of the deck, the five cards having been arranged so that the lowest was on top and the highest second in line. As she did this she gave the five cards a quick, almost imperceptible squeeze, which produced a slight convex longitudinal bend. During the shuffle, she maneuvered the five-card slug to the top of the deck. Then, just before offering the deck for the cut, she buried the slug in the middle, at the point where her opponent tended to cut each time. The slight crimp in the cards ensured that the slug would be returned to the top. All she had to do then was to deal fairly, flexing the deck once or twice first to take out the slug's bend. The first card she dealt, which she knew from memory, was therefore the opponent's hole card. And her hole card, the second in line, was always higher.

"Clever," John said. "The advantage is small, but for a sharp it's enough to control almost any game."

Sabina dipped her chin in agreement. "But I'll need to play her once more—or rather, the Saint Louis Rose will—to make absolutely sure I'm right about her gaff. An hour or so should do it. If, that is, Mr. McFinn will stake me to another five hundred."

"He will if you tell him what you suspect."

"I'm not sure I should until I'm certain. And he was already bemoaning the loss of tonight's fifteen hundred."

"He agreed to finance your gambling. Another five hundred won't matter to him if his star attraction is quietly exposed as a cheat and it saves the Gold Nugget from being shut down." The broad wink again. "Of course, if he does refuse I could finance the Rose's game myself in exchange for her favors."

His boldness had increased since she had allowed him to keep company with her outside the office, and in a weak moment had gone with him to his bachelor flat one evening after dinner, and as always it exasperated her. There was a time and place for such forward banter, and while they were engaged in an undercover investigation was neither of those. She said as much, sternly. He pretended to pout, but had the good sense not to make any further unwelcome comments.

"To get back to business," Sabina said, "I don't intend to lose to Lady One-Eye again tomorrow night. I know ways to counteract her trick, thanks to Jim Moon."

"At any rate, if you're convinced, we'll put an end to the matter as soon as the game is finished. The sooner McFinn sends her packing, the better off he'll be. There's more trouble afoot than the possibility of someone else with a keen eye tumbling to the Lady's trick."

"What do you mean? Jack O'Diamonds' attentions to Lily Dumont?"

"Yes. And the overprotectiveness of Jeffrey Gaunt, a gent I wish I knew more about."

"I could make some discreet inquiries in the morning. As discreet as the Saint Louis Rose is likely to be, that is."

"A good idea. Anything else the Rose can find out, too, especially regarding Diamond's affair with Lily and the threatening note." He paused before adding, "It's more than possible now that the threat is genuine."

"Now? Has something happened?"

"At Lily's cottage half an hour ago. Two rounds from a heavy revolver nearly took my head off."

"John! Someone tried to kill you? Who?"

"I didn't get a look at him. Or her. Too dark."

"There was no light where you were?"

"No."

"Then whoever it was couldn't see you clearly, either."

"Only a dark shape as I left the cottage," John said. "If you're thinking he might have mistaken me for someone else, you're right, I may not have been the intended target."

"Jack O'Diamonds?"

"Or Lily. Or Glen Bonnifield, if it wasn't Bonnifield who did the shooting."

"Is he the reason you went to her cottage?"

"One of them. Lily's involvement with Diamond seems more than a simple dalliance. It occurred to me that she might have written the note."

"Why her?" Sabina asked. "What would she hope to gain by it? Unless—"

"Unless Diamond and Lily are in cahoots, the addition of his name to the note was a red herring, and the plan not an attempt to drive Lady One-Eye away but to pave the way for her murder. In that case, the blame would be attached to the anonymous letter writer, a deranged local, and no suspicion would fall on them."

"Did you find evidence to incriminate her?"

"None. No bottle of green ink."

Sabina said thoughtfully, "If Bonnifield is the jealous sort he seems to be, *he* could be the author of the note."

"He could, though he doesn't strike me as the type to resort to written warnings. He was in the Gold Nugget tonight, glaring daggers at both Lily and Jack."

"Yes, I noticed. I don't like that shooting business tonight, John. You're right that it portends more serious trouble than we first believed."

"We had both better be on our guard tomorrow," he said. "Take your derringer along to the Gold Nugget, just in case."

"It's already handy in my bag." She couldn't resist adding, "And knowing that, aren't you glad you didn't foolishly try to kiss me and take me to bed just now?"

When she was alone again, Sabina finished divesting herself of the rest of her doxy's costume, put on her nightgown, and got into bed. It was a feather bed and she sank into it gratefully. But despite the lateness of the hour, her weariness after the long, intense poker match with Lady One-Eye, sleep eluded her. Her thoughts roamed here and there, first over the complicated nature of their investigation, then on John and their relationship.

For their first five years as partners in Carpenter and Quincannon, Professional Detective Services, she had insisted on a strict business-only policy, fending off his periodic advances with ease for she believed his only personal interest in her was the typical male's: seduction and conquest. Likely that was the case in the beginning, but his intentions had gradually changed, his feelings for her growing more respectful, deepening into the kind of affection that, if not exactly love, is the next thing to it. His campaign to take her to bed was now something quite differently motivated, she was sure—the passion of a man eager for a long-term liaison, perhaps even marriage.

Her own feelings for him had changed, too, softened in return. But just how tender she still wasn't sure. She could never love any man as she had loved Stephen, yet there were different kinds, different degrees of love. For five years now she had remained faithful to Stephen's memory, but she was a healthy woman in the prime of her life. It would be easy enough to succumb to John's advances—she had come close, very close, that night at his flat after the one long, passionate kiss she had permitted (and, yes, greatly enjoyed)—but she'd promised herself she would not give herself to him unless he asked for her hand in marriage.

Would her answer be yes if he did? She wasn't quite sure, perhaps wouldn't be until, if, and when. Would she consent to sleep with him even if her answer were no? She wasn't quite sure of that, either, although his kisses, particularly the one that night in his flat, had awakened feelings in her that had lain dormant for five long years . . .

4

SABINA

In the morning she spent the better part of half an hour once again turning herself into the Saint Louis Rose.

First she pinned up her hair, then carefully applied pancake makeup and rouge—just enough of both to enhance the somewhat bawdy appearance of a lady gambler without crossing the line into that of a strumpet. The false eyelashes were appropriate enough at night, but in the daylight they would be grotesque; she left them off. Although her svelte figure had no real need of a corset, she wriggled her way into the one she'd brought and tightened the straps. In deference to the summer heat, she donned the lightest of her three Rose costumes, a yellow silk dress with a bosom cut somewhat less boldly low than her evening attire. She had a little trouble with the red wig. Dratted thing wouldn't fit as it should, requiring a number of repinnings.

She smiled with wry satisfaction at the image of herself, or rather of the Saint Louis Rose, in the gold-framed wall mirror. She really did enjoy this sort of playacting, but only on a limited basis. How professional actresses could endure all the time and effort necessary to prepare for regular performances was beyond her.

It was a quarter of nine when Sabina shouldered the folded, gaily colored parasol, the final fillip to her costume, and left the room, locking the door behind her. John had told her he would be taking the Nevada County Narrow Gauge train to Nevada City early this morning, so there was no need to stop at his room. They had arranged to meet at three P.M. on the City Hall green to discuss the day's inquiries.

She descended the staircase to the lobby. The young desk clerk watched with avid eyes as she crossed to the dining room. She favored him with a smile and a broad, bold wink that caused him to blush noticeably and avert his gaze. Oh, what a wicked wench the Saint Louis Rose was! Nothing at all like the proper, well-bred Sabina Carpenter.

Among the several people having breakfast in the dining room were Lady One-Eye and Jeffrey Gaunt. It was no surprise to find them there; the Holbrooke's dining facilities were open to the public and they reportedly served the best fare in Grass Valley. The poker sharp wore either the same long-sleeved black dress as the night before or its twin; her brother was also garbed in his usual black frock coat and striped gray trousers—an outfit that put Sabina in mind of a mortician. They were presently engaged in what, judging from their expressions, was a rather intense conversation. Sabina detoured to a stop alongside their table.

"Good morning, Mr. Gaunt. Hello, dearie."

Gaunt nodded, Lady One-Eye fixed her with her Cyclopian stare. Neither of them spoke.

"Mind if I join you?"

"Yes, we do mind," Lady-One Eye said in her icy drawl. "Find someone else to annoy."

"You'll find me more than annoying when we play poker again tonight, dearie, for I'll be the one to do the trimming."

"Like hell you will."

Sabina laughed. "Such language from an alleged lady," she said mockingly, and hip-swayed to an empty table not far away.

Gaunt and Lady One-Eye resumed their conversation, in voices too low for Sabina to hear. They seemed to be at odds about something, she tight-lipped with evident anger, he calm and stoic. The attention Jack O'Diamonds was paying to Lily Dumont, perhaps?

A waitress brought Sabina's breakfast order: two eggs, a large slice of ham, bread and butter, coffee. An expense-account meal, not that paying for it herself would have deterred her. Thank goodness she was blessed with a metabolism to match her considerable appetite. Unlike most other women she knew past the age of thirty, she never gained weight no matter how much she ate or how rich the food.

She was mopping up the last of the egg yolk with a morsel of bread when Lady One-Eye abruptly shoved back her chair, levered herself upright, and limped out with the support of her gold-knobbed cane. Gaunt remained seated, watching his sister until she disappeared into the lobby. Then he removed a small, black ledger book from the inside pocket of his coat and began making pencil notations in it.

Sabina dabbed at her mouth with her cloth napkin, stood, adjusted her dress, and once again approached Gaunt's table. Without being invited, she sat down in the chair Lady One-Eye had occupied. "Toting up your sister's winnings from last night?" she asked.

He sat back, regarding her with his frosty blue eyes. "That is no concern of yours."

"Yes it is, since a fair lot of that money was mine until the last hand. It will be mine again tonight, plus a good deal more."

"So you stated earlier." Gaunt closed the ledger book, returned it to his coat pocket. "I wouldn't be so confident if I were you, Miss Rose."

"Miss Rose. Hoo! I do like a courtly Southern gentleman."

Gaunt said nothing. The deep, wide cleft in his chin was somewhat disconcerting when seen up close like this. On most men such a cleft would have been an attractive feature, but not on him. It gave his face a different kind of sinister cast from his sister's, as if a hole had been bored below his mouth, or a bullet had once been lodged there and dug out to leave a crater.

"Are you and the Lady from New Orleans?" Sabina asked.

"Who told you that?"

"No one. Your accents suggest it. Not so?"

"Louisiana, yes. N'Orleans, no. Baton Rouge."

"But your sister's played her share of poker in the Vieux Carré, no doubt, same as I have. On the Mississippi River packets, too—I expect that's where Jack O'Diamonds once did much of his gambling. Surprising our paths never crossed until now."

"Yes, isn't it."

"But I'm known as the Saint Louis Rose for good reason. That city was my home base for some time before I came west. The Lady and Jack do much business in the Missouri Belle or any of the other Saint Louie parlors?"

"Some."

"Must have been before my time," Sabina said. "Where else has she plied her talents?"

"Various places."

"Austin? San Antonio? Tombstone?"

"Various places, as I said."

"Where are you bound after Grass Valley? Another town in the Mother Lode? San Francisco?"

"That hasn't been decided yet."

"But you will be on your way soon?"

"You think so? Why?"

"The kettle's getting a bit hot here, wouldn't you say?"

"No, I wouldn't. Why should you think that?"

"I have eyes, mister. Good, sharp eyes."

Gaunt refused to take the bait. "You're quite inquisitive, aren't you, Miss Rose," he said flatly.

"I like to know who I'm dealing with. Especially when I've been trimmed as neatly as I was last night."

"That is the second time this morning you have used the word 'trimmed.' I don't care for your inference."

"What inference?"

"That my sister is anything but an extremely skilled poker player."

"Well, now, the thought did cross my mind."

Gaunt's mustache twitched. "Lady One-Eye has no need of trickery," he said. "She is in a class by herself."

"Oh? Has she ever sat at table with Poker Alice?"

"Not yet. It will be a match for the ages when she does."

"If she does. And if she's as honest as you claim she is. Poker Alice would spot a mechanic straightaway, no matter how skilled her gaff."

"So would you, I should think, if you possess the credentials *you* claim to have."

"I've been fooled before by expert mechanics, but not for long. I intend to keep an extra sharp eye on the cards when the Lady and I play tonight."

Gaunt's piercing gaze remained fixed on her for several more seconds. Then, abruptly, without so much as a by-your-leave, he pushed to his feet and walked out.

There was no sign of Jack O'Diamonds, Lily Dumont, or Lady One-Eye when Sabina entered the Gold Nugget. One of the bartenders told her that Amos McFinn was in his office.

The little man was in his usual jittery state. "It's about time you reported, Mrs. Carpenter. I—"

"The Saint Louis Rose," she reminded him.

"Yes, yes, there's no one else here. Well? What's your

opinion of Lady One-Eye's game after losing to her last night? Is she honest or not?"

"I'd rather not say just yet. I'll have to play her once more before I can be sure."

"But you think she may be a clever sharp, is that it?"

"You'll have my answer tonight, Mr. McFinn. Another hour at table with her ought to be sufficient, win or lose. For which I'll need an additional stake."

McFinn made a groaning sound. "How much this time?"

"Five hundred."

"For a total of two thousand if you lose again and she's honest."

"And full restitution if she's not."

He went to a large Mosler safe behind his desk, removed five hundred dollars in greenbacks. "I'd rather forfeit the two thousand," he muttered as he handed the money to Sabina. "My house percentage on her winnings already amounts to twice as much."

Sabina tucked the bills into her bag without comment.

"Do you have anything else to report?" McFinn asked.

"Again, not yet. I had a conversation with Jeffrey Gaunt a few minutes ago, but it yielded nothing of import."

"He didn't say anything about that damned . . . the threatening letter?"

"No. The Saint Louis Rose has no way of knowing about it, and he wouldn't bring it up to her in any case. Nor would he be drawn into a discussion of Jack O'Diamonds' infatuation with Lily Dumont."

"Quincannon mentioned his suspicion of an affair last

night," McFinn said. "I asked the girl about it this morning, straight-out."

"She denied the involvement, of course."

"In no uncertain terms."

"And you believed her?"

"She . . . well, she seemed sincere."

"Glen Bonnifield, Lady One-Eye, and her brother all seem to suspect infidelity. As do John and I. If we're correct, it makes the situation even more volatile and potentially violent."

McFinn groaned again. "As if I need anything more to worry about."

He would have been all the more fretted if Sabina had told him about the shooting at Lily Dumont's cottage. The decision she and John had made not to reveal it yet was the right one.

"You and your partner had better get to the bottom of things in a hurry. Where is he today, by the way? I haven't seen him since he left at the end of his shift last night."

"In Nevada City."

"Doing what?"

"The same as I'll be doing today and tonight," Sabina said. "What you're paying us to do—investigate."

She spent the rest of the morning once again asking veiled questions of various habitués of the Gold Nugget and Grass Valley's other gaming parlors, seeking information on locals whose anti-gambling sentiments were strong enough to have resulted in the threatening letter, and on the activities past and present of Lady One-Eye, Jack O'Diamonds, and Jeffrey

Gaunt. One of those she wanted to speak to, but didn't, was Lily Dumont; the faro dealer was nowhere to be found at her cottage, in the parlors, or anywhere else in town.

She learned nothing of significance.

After she had her midday meal at a fairly good restaurant, the humid summer heat drove her back to the relatively cool confines of the Holbrooke Hotel. As she entered the lobby, she thought—not for the first time—what a curious coincidence it was to have undertaken a case that brought her to Grass Valley and the Holbrooke. For they were where Carson Montgomery had worked as a young metallurgist in the rough-and-ready boom years of Nevada County gold mining.

It had been during that period that Carson committed the transgression that left him open to blackmail and threatened his successful career as a mining engineer—a dark secret uncovered by Sabina that had led to the end of their brief romance less than a year ago. She hadn't seen him since. Although she was not sorry they'd parted company, she retained pleasant memories of the interlude and wished him well. And from what she'd read in the newspapers' social columns, he had recovered from the incident quite nicely: he was now engaged to the daughter of a wealthy stockbroker.

The thought of Carson led naturally, as she ascended the staircase to the second floor, to Charles Percival Fairchild III. It had been Charles the Third who had learned of the blackmail attempt and alerted her to it. The daft but shrewdly clever fellow who fancied himself to be the great detective Sherlock Holmes, but who was in fact scion to a Chicago meatpacking fortune, had for nearly a year skulked among the denizens of

San Francisco's underworld and insinuated himself into several of her and John's cases, often with startling results. He could be highly annoying, with his secretive ways and outlandish disguises, yet also quite charming and helpful. And the last time she'd seen him, at the close of the Plague of Thieves Affair in January, he had literally saved her life.

He had left the city shortly afterward, to avoid the police and legal ramifications, and hadn't been heard from or about since. She wondered again what had become of him. Had he returned to England, where he'd lived in self-exile for several years? To Chicago, to claim his father's inheritance despite the unshakable conviction that he was Sherlock Holmes, Esquire? To some other city, where he was now continuing to indulge his delusion? She would have liked to know; in spite of herself she almost missed having him around. Not so, John, however. Charles had been a thorn in his side too long, upstaging him on more than one occasion with some rather amazing detective work and earning his everlasting enmity . . .

In her room, she pulled the cord to the ceiling fan, then removed the itchy wig, slipped out of Rose's dress, and lay down on the bed. Afternoon naps were a luxury she hardly ever had the time or inclination to indulge in in the city. Here, one was a necessity as well as a relief, given the likely stresses of the evening ahead.

Her internal clock woke her after forty-five minutes. Another fifteen were sufficient to refresh her guise as the Saint Louis Rose. The clock in the lobby read 2:50 when she left the hotel to keep her three o'clock appointment with John on the City Hall green.

5

QUINCANNON

Nevada City, three miles to the east, was likewise a gold-mining town. It had been founded during the first year of the Gold Rush, Quincannon knew, two years before Grass Valley was settled. Its first and largest mine, the Gold Tunnel on the north side of Deer Creek, had made it the richest mining town in the state during that period. Grass Valley's Empire and North Star mines had eventually surpassed the Gold Tunnel's output, and siphoned off some of Nevada City's population of miners and their families. But the amount of gold-bearing ore produced here remained substantial enough to the present day to support the local economy.

Quincannon spent the better part of four hours making the rounds of the saloons and gaming parlors—one of them Glen Bonnifield's Ace High—and local merchant establishments, pretending to be a patent-medicine drummer and asking seemingly casual questions. He learned several things about

Bonnifield and the saloon owner's relationship with Lily Dumont, a few of potential significance.

The slow NCNG train deposited him back in Grass Valley a few minutes past two o'clock. From the depot, he walked up heat-glazed, semi-deserted East Main to the Gold Nugget.

In the harsh glare of sunlight, the exterior of the gambling hall had an uninviting aspect. Like nearly all of the commercial buildings here, it been constructed of brick—the consequence of a disastrous fire in 1855 that had consumed the township's three hundred wooden structures, leaving nothing standing but Wells Fargo's brick-and-iron vault and a dozen scorched brick chimneys. The massive sign above the door had a warped and faded look; the brass fittings of the red-globed lamps were pitted with rust. Little wonder, Quincannon thought, that the bluenoses were bent on closing it and its sisters down. Some of the other gambling resorts here and in Nevada City had even tawdrier appearances by daylight.

At this hour there were relatively few customers. All but two of the gaming tables were covered, Lily Dumont's faro bank among them. There was no sign of the buxom Lily, nor of Lady One-Eye, Jack O'Diamonds, or Jeffrey Gaunt. Amos McFinn hovered behind the bar, looking harried as usual. Quincannon went to the unoccupied end and McFinn, spying him, hurried over.

"Well?" the little man demanded without preamble. "Did you find out anything today?"

"Nothing to be confided just yet, Mr. McFinn."

"Damn! That is just what your compatriot—"

Quincannon said warningly, "I have no compatriot here."

"The Saint Louis Rose, I meant to say. Just what she said when I spoke to her earlier."

"Not a wise idea to be questioning her. You'll upset the apple cart if you're not careful."

"She came to see me. We spoke privately in my office. She claims to be able to tell me tonight whether or not Lady One-Eye is cheating."

"And so she will."

"Are you sure she knows the game of poker well enough to be absolutely certain?"

"Better than you or I, and as well as Lady One-Eye," Quincannon assured him. "You needn't worry. Your money is being well spent."

"That remains to be seen," McFinn said dolefully.

Sabina was waiting on a tree-shaded bench on the Stewart Street side of City Hall, her open parasol providing additional insulation from the blazing afternoon sun. The bright yellow summer dress she wore, he was relieved to note as he strolled up, revealed less of her charms than her evening attire. He sat down beside her, fanned himself with his derby. There was no one else in the vicinity except for a heat-flattened mongrel dog stretched out asleep behind the bench.

Sabina looked a bit on the wilted side herself, and he made the mistake of saying so.

"You'd be wilted, too, if you had to wear this infernal wig," she said crossly. "I should have had the sense not to bother covering my own hair with such a contrivance."

"Then we would have had to name you the Saint Louis Black."

"I am in no mood for badinage, John. Was your trip to Nevada City worthwhile?"

"Up to a point. Glen Bonnifield is in fact keeping Lily in her cottage and has been for more than a year. He has an evidently justifiable reputation for jealousy and an explosive temper. Last year he threatened to shoot a man who had been pestering her. And he carries a Colt Peacemaker and is reported to be an excellent shot."

"A dangerous man. And likely the one who shot at you at Lily's cottage last night."

Quincannon nodded agreement. "A hothead of direct action, not devious design. Would such a man write a note forewarning both a rival and the rival's wife?"

"No."

"No, indeed. So was it Jack O'Diamonds who wrote the note, to pave the way for a murder plot against Lady One-Eye devised by him alone or with the collusion of Lily Dumont? Or was its author, after all, some anti-gambling individual who might or might not intend to carry out his threat?"

"Rhetorical questions, John."

"So you learned nothing that might point in either direction?"

"Nothing more than yesterday. The anti-gambling faction here has more than a few ardent members. If the note was written by one of them there's no way to identify him—or her—short of asking for sample handwriting from every local resident."

"Faugh."

She told him of the intense breakfast-table discussion between Lady One-Eye and Jeffrey Gaunt, and of her own conversation with Gaunt. "Unless I miss my guess," she said, "the brother-and-sister discussion concerned Jack O'Diamonds and Lily Dumont."

"It would explain Lady One-Eye's anger. Did Gaunt seem upset beneath his calm demeanor?"

"I would say he was," Sabina said. "He is certainly aware of the affair, if their infatuation with each other has gone that far."

"There seems little doubt that it has. Does he strike you as capable of violence to preserve his sister's alleged honor?"

"As capable of it as Bonnifield, if I'm any judge of men."

Oh, you are, Quincannon thought, and none better at it, I'll warrant. "A bad situation, in any case. One I have a feeling may soon come to a head. But how soon?"

"Yes," Sabina said, "and where and in what way?"

At five o'clock, in fresh clothing and with a plate of liver and onions residing more or less comfortably within, Quincannon returned to the Gold Nugget to resume his duties behind the bar.

Lily Dumont was there, setting up her faro bank. No one was with her, and when a bearded miner drifted over and attempted to start a conversation, she brushed him off with a sharp word. She seemed preoccupied—and almost as nervous as McFinn. Quincannon wondered if the cause of her agitation was that she'd gotten wind of the shooting last night.

Lady One-Eye and Jack O'Diamonds arrived together, but soon parted without a word to each other. The Lady took her place at the platform table and was immediately challenged by a pair of whiskered gents who had the look of nouveau riche prospectors. Diamond made his way to the bar, where he drank two brandies in short order. Then he moved restlessly about the room, stopping for a time to play vingt-et-un and then again to play faro. But it was not Lily's bank that he chose. He avoided going anywhere near her, as if she were not even on the premises. Lily, likewise, paid not the slightest attention to him. A falling-out of some sort? Or part of a plan that might have been hatched between them?

The last to arrive was Jeffrey Gaunt, dressed in his customary rusty black suit and string tie, his pomaded hair glistening in the lamplight. He sat alone at the same table he'd occupied the night before, where he alternately watched his sister play, cast long, hard looks in the direction of his brother-in-law, and made notations in his ledger book.

The Saint Louis Rose made her entrance shortly afterward, wearing a frilly green outfit with a low-cut bodice that struck Quincannon as even more revealing than last night's scarlet number. Where had she gotten such clothing? From a costumers, probably, though she hadn't said so. For all he knew she had a closet full of such apparel and had been leading a wanton double life, slipping out once or twice a week to Barbary Coast deadfalls. Hah! Fanciful notion if ever there was one.

Still, there were hidden depths in her, of that he was sure—a wanton within a proper lady, waiting to be released. That thought, in spite of the time and place, quickened his blood. It also put him in mind of a quatrain from a poem by Emily Dickinson.

Wild Nights! Wild Nights!
Were I with thee,
Wild Nights should be
Our luxury!

He sighed as he watched her sashay across the room, drawing admiring and lustful looks from the early-gathered customers. It made him testy to see the men ogling her in such a fashion. As if he were a jealous husband.

She joined Jack O'Diamonds at the faro table, attempted to engage him in conversation. The gambler spurned her; he seemed as preoccupied as Lily Dumont. Three times in less than an hour he ordered brandy from one of the percentage girls. But the liquor seemed to have little or no effect on him.

Lady One-Eye made short work of the two Cornish miners, taking a hundred dollars from one and twice that amount from another. They accepted their losses more or less good-naturedly, the biggest loser offering to buy her a magnum of champagne as a token of his esteem for her skills. She declined. There was a tight set to her mouth tonight, a distracted mechanical quality to her movements.

Shortly after the prospectors left Lady One-Eye alone on the platform, Glen Bonnifield walked in. Or, more precisely, weaved in. His face was dark flushed, his eyes blood flecked, his expression brooding: the look of a man who had spent a good part of the day in close company with a bottle of whiskey. Trouble afoot, all right, Quincannon thought darkly, and no gainsaying it.

Bonnifield lurched up to his station, stood for a few seconds glowering in the direction of Lily Dumont. Then he called for rye.

Quincannon said politely, "Carrying a bit of a load tonight, eh, Mr. Bonnifield?"

"What if I am? No concern of yours."

"No, sir, except that you forgot to check your weapon."

"My what?"

"The Peacemaker poking out from under your coat."

"No *damn* concern of yours," Bonnifield growled. He spat into one of the knee-high cuspidors. "Pour my rye, barkeep, and be quick about it."

"Not until you obey the rules of the house and check your weapon."

"Well, now. Why don't you try checking it for me?"

His voice was loud, belligerent; some of the other patrons swung their heads to stare at him. So did Lily Dumont. When she saw the condition he was in, her nervousness escalated into visible fright.

"Let's not have an altercation, Mr. Bonnifield."

"There'll be an altercation, all right, by God. But not with the likes of you."

Abruptly Bonnifield shoved away from the rail, staggered

over to Lily's faro bank. She shrank back while two of her customers moved out of harm's way. Quincannon was on the move through the notch in the bar by then. He heard McFinn shout a warning to his bouncers; he also glimpsed Jack O'Diamonds jump up and start past the raised platform to Lily's defense.

What remained of Bonnifield's self-control had dissolved in drunken fury. He yelled, "You little tramp, I won't let you make a fool out of me!" and his hand groped under his coat for the Peacemaker.

Quincannon reached the saloonkeeper just as he drew the big-barreled weapon, knocked his arm down before he could trigger a shot. Bonnifield swung wildly with his other hand, struck Quincannon's shoulder a glancing blow that drove him backward on his heels. Two of the bouncers muscled up, grabbed hold of the saloonkeeper, and tried to wrestle him into submission. He broke free and stumbled into a confused group of customers and Gold Nugget employees, still clutching his Peacemaker. Men shouted; a woman let out a shrill cry of alarm.

And in the midst of all this ferment, a single pistol shot sounded, low and popping, like the explosion of a Fourth of July firecracker.

A man grunted loudly in pain. That and the report ended the budding melee, parted the crowd in a fashion that was almost biblical. Quincannon saw a number of things in that instant. He saw the two bouncers drive Bonnifield to the floor and disarm him. He saw Lily rush away from her faro bank, Jeffrey Gaunt do the same from his table. He saw Sabina running toward him. He saw Lady One-Eye seated at her poker table, one hand on the green baize and the other at the bodice of her dress. And in the cleared space where the mass of people had fallen back on both sides, he saw the victim of the gunshot lying supine and motionless, blood staining his vest at heart level.

"It's Jack!" Lily shrieked. "Oh, no, it's *Jack*!"

6

SABINA

Sabina rushed up just as Lily Dumont flung herself to her knees beside the inert form of Jack O'Diamonds, laid her flame-colored head against his chest. When she lifted it again, her eyes were wet with tears. "He's not breathing," she wailed, "he's dead."

Lady One-Eye, Sabina saw, was standing stock-still next to her table, her body stiff, her mouth clamped tight. Her good eye blazed with cold fire, but her set expression seemed void of sorrow, anger, even shock. Her brother, bunched among the miners and sports staring down at the dead man, showed no emotion of any kind; his face was as blank as a piece of slate. There had been no love lost between him and Jack O'Diamonds, Sabina thought, the two men barely on speaking terms, at least in public. Because of Diamond's affair with Lily Dumont, or for some other reason?

Amos McFinn was bellowing to his bouncers to seal off the

front and rear entrances, keep everybody inside the hall. To an extent, fortunately, this had already been done. One of the bouncers, a massive fellow with the bulging biceps of a blacksmith, had taken up a post at the front entrance and was not allowing anyone to leave or enter. The others rushed to obey their employer's command.

Lily drew back from her lover's body, and two of the men moved to help her to her feet. Immediately she shook a clenched fist at Glen Bonnifield, who was down on one knee a few feet away. "You did it! Damn you, Glen, *you* killed him!"

Bonnifield appeared dazed from his scuffle with the bouncers; if he heard her he made no reply. One of the miners held the Peacemaker Bonnifield had drawn at Lily's faro bank. John stepped over to him, took the weapon and felt and then sniffed the barrel.

"Not with this, he didn't," he said. "It hasn't been fired."

McFinn came dancing up, his eyes as wide as a toad's. "Then who did shoot him?" he demanded. "Quincannon, did you see who pulled the trigger?"

John admitted that he hadn't. He glanced at Sabina; she responded with a slight shake of her head.

"Did *anyone* see who fired that shot?" the little man roared.

No one had. Or at least no one would own up to having witnessed the shooting.

Lady One-Eye had hobbled down off the platform, pushed her way through the crowd, and was pointing her cane at the remains of Jack O'Diamonds. "Look there," she said. "Some blackguard not only murdered my husband, he stole Jack's diamond stickpin."

She sounded more upset over the loss of his stickpin than she did over the loss of his life.

Sheriff Hezekiah Thorpe was a man in his early fifties, with a tawny soup-strainer mustache and an efficient, no-nonsense manner. He took charge as soon as he and two of his deputies arrived with the man McFinn had dispatched to bring them.

The answers to a few terse questions allowed him to separate the principal players in the drama from the extras and on-lookers, none of whom had been allowed to leave the hall. No one admitted to having witnessed the shooting. Thorpe and his deputies searched the men, Quincannon included, and then the rest of the assembled patrons and employees. Four hideout pistols were the result, but not one of those had been fired, either. Nor was the murder weapon anywhere to be found on the premises.

The sheriff and one of the deputies herded Sabina, John, and the other principals into McFinn's private quarters at the rear. The single exception was Glen Bonnifield. One of the bouncers had fetched him a crack on the head with a billy club in order to subdue him after he drew his Peacemaker, and Bonnifield still had not regained his wits. He was being administered to by a town doctor.

Suspense crackled among the small group. Lily Dumont continued to shed tears—genuine tears, Sabina judged—and Lady One-Eye once again wore her stoic poker face. But it was plain that neither she nor Lily, nor the equally stoic Jeffrey Gaunt, were pleased to learn that a pair of San Francisco detectives had been operating undercover in their midst, the reasons for which having yet to be divulged. The recent widow kept casting glacial looks at Sabina (who had shed her itchy Saint Louis Rose wig once her true identity was revealed), the looks a measure of her resentment at having been duped by a disguised woman investigator who was also her equal at the poker table. McFinn was still in a lather. He kept glaring at John with open hostility, as if John were somehow responsible for the death of Jack O'Diamonds in his establishment.

They had met Thorpe on their arrival in Grass Valley; it was always wise for private inquiry agents hired to operate undercover in foreign territory to make themselves known to the local constabulary, in order to avoid any potential conflict. The sheriff had been friendly enough then, but the friendliness was in abeyance now. There was an edge to his voice as he said, "Can you sort out for us what took place here tonight, Mr. Quincannon?"

"He couldn't sort out a handful of poker chips," McFinn snapped. His habitual nervousness had given way to outrage. "Neither him nor his lady partner. I hired them to keep disaster from my door and they failed miserably. The publicity from this will give the bluenoses all the ammunition they need to close the Gold Nugget down. I'll be ruined—"

"Amos, hold your tongue."

"I still say Glen Bonnifield shot poor Jack," Lily said before John could respond. "He hated him, he made no bones about that. And last night . . . I was told by a neighbor that shots were fired at my cottage. That must have been Glen, too, after Jack."

"Diamond was at your cottage last night?"

"No. I wasn't there, either, when it happened. But Glen must've thought we'd gone there together."

"Why would he shoot at an empty cottage?"

John said carefully, "It may be that he was hiding outside and mistook a shadow for a man." He cast a glance at Sabina as he spoke, not that she needed to be warned to keep silent. She knew as well as he did that declaring he was a mistaken target would serve no purpose except to vex the sheriff. He had, after all, entered Lily's home illegally; and he had also failed to report the shooting.

Thorpe asked him, "So then you also think Bonnifield killed Jack Diamond?"

"No. I suspect it was Bonnifield who fired those shots last night, but he had nothing to do with what happened here."

"How do you know he didn't?"

"You examined his weapon, just as I did. He must have cleaned it after using it last night—it hadn't been fired tonight. Also, the report of a Peacemaker is loud, booming. The shot that folded Jack O'Diamonds was low and popping, like that of a firecracker."

"A small-caliber weapon, then."

"Yes. A derringer or a pocket revolver."

"Does Bonnifield carry a hideout weapon, Miss Dumont?"

"No. I've never seen one."

"And if he did have one tonight," John pointed out, "he had no time to rid himself of it."

"Then who did shoot Diamond?"

"Not my sister or me," Jeffrey Gaunt said, speaking for the first time. "Neither of us has ever carried a weapon."

"Did Diamond?"

"On occasion, yes. A double-barreled derringer."

"Well, it wasn't on his body." Thorpe turned to Lady One-Eye. "When did you last see it, Mrs. Diamond?"

"I don't recall," she said. "If he wasn't carrying it, I expect you'll find it among his belongings in our lodgings."

"Someone could have stolen it and used it to shoot him."

"Yes, but who? And who stole his diamond stickpin?"

John said, "I can answer that question."

"Oh, you can," Thorpe said. "Who?"

John's penchant for the dramatic led him to pause before responding. He lifted a hand and would have fluffed his beard if it were still untrimmed. As it was he settled for clearing his throat several times.

"Lily Dumont, of course," he said.

"Her! I should've known." Lady One-Eye jabbed menacingly at the younger woman with her cane. "You dirty, murdering husband-stealer—"

Lily shrank away from her. "It's a lie! I didn't kill Jack and I didn't steal his stickpin."

"Ah, but you did," John said. "Slipped it out of his cravat when you flung yourself down beside his body, in the moment before you announced that he was dead. You were the only person close enough to have managed it without being noticed."

Sabina said wryly, "Jack O'Diamonds' handsome face wasn't his only lure for her. Money and the promise of more to come was at least part of the reason she was going away with him."

"What's that?" Thorpe said. "She was going away with Diamond?"

"All right," Lily cried, "all right, I was. And yes, I took his stickpin—why shouldn't I? He was dead and he would've wanted me to have it. He loved me and I loved him."

Lady One-Eye uttered a coarse word well known to cattle-men. "I want it back. Where is it?"

"Where you'll never find it."

"You didn't have time to hide it. It's still on your person. I'll strip you naked right here in front of these men if you don't give it up."

The threat, Sabina thought, was not an idle one. Lily knew it, too. She bit her lip, turned her back, and fished the stick-pin from the bodice of her dress. Lady One-Eye reached for it, but Thorpe claimed it first.

"Evidence," he said.

Lily appealed to him, saying, "But I *didn't* shoot him. You have to believe me. I don't own a handgun, I don't even know how to fire one."

The sheriff turned to John. "Is she telling the truth or not?"

John cleared his throat again, but not for the same reason as before, and tugged at his shirt collar as if it had grown a tad snug. The gesture almost made Sabina smile. She knew him well enough by now to know when his deductive prowess had temporarily failed him: he had no clear-cut idea of who had fired the fatal shot.

"Ah, perhaps she is," he hedged, "and then again perhaps she isn't."

"What the devil does that mean?"

"It means," McFinn said scornfully, "he doesn't know either way. He doesn't have a clue to the identity of Diamond's murderer."

There was a small uncomfortable silence.

The time had come for Sabina to step in. She said, "Of course he does. We both know the murderer's name and how the crime was committed. Don't we, John?"

He blinked at her. There had been a time in the early years of their professional relationship when he'd considered her a very competent detective though not his equal when it came to solving the knottier type of problem. That attitude had since changed, fortunately for both their sakes or they would not have reached the level of intimacy they presently shared. The look he gave her now not only showed gratitude for her face-saving gesture, but both respect and eagerness.

"Well, Mrs. Carpenter?" Thorpe demanded. "Who was it?"

"Lady One-Eye, of course."

Heads swung toward the recent widow. Lady One-Eye stood in her usual ramrod-stiff posture, one hand resting on the gold knob of her cane, her good eye impaling Sabina. The only emotion it or her expression betrayed was contempt.

"How dare you accuse me. I might have been shot, too, to-night. Or have you forgotten the note that threatened my life and my husband's?"

"I haven't forgotten it. You wrote that note yourself."

"*I* wrote it? That's ridiculous."

"On the contrary," Sabina said. "When we were about to play stud tonight I noticed a faint smudge of green on your left thumb—green ink, the same color as the writing on the note, that multiple hand-washings was unable to eradicate. My guess is that you didn't bother to dispose of the bottle and the sheriff will find it in your lodgings."

"Suppose she did write the note," Thorpe said. "What was her purpose?"

Lady One-Eye said, "Yes, whatever your name is, what possible reason could I have for threatening myself and shooting my husband?"

"He was going to leave you, that's why!" Lily cried. The shift of suspicion from her to her rival had relieved her, made her bold again. "He was tired of you and your cold and stingy ways. And you knew it."

"I knew nothing of the kind. Did I, Jeffrey?"

"Certainly not," her brother said, his slow drawl as wintery as hers. "Nor did I, for it isn't true."

Lily pointed a tremulous finger at Lady One-Eye. "Oh, yes it is. You as much as said so last night at my table. You warned me against trying to take Jack away from you."

"If that were true, which it wasn't, and I were going to shoot anyone, it would have been *you*, not him."

"Unless," Sabina said, "your hate for him and his faithless ways had become intolerable, as it surely had. He must have let something slip earlier today that convinced you he was going to run off with Lily, and soon, perhaps as soon as tonight."

"Yes," Lily said. "Tonight!"

"With her and possibly some or all of your recent winnings."

"Utter claptrap," Gaunt said. He laid a protective hand on

Lady One-Eye's arm, glaring daggers at Sabina as he did so. "I have complete control of my sister's finances. There is no way Jack could have gotten his hands on any of her money."

She ignored him. "That's why you acted when you did," she said to Lady One-Eye. "As for the note, you wrote that to divert suspicion from yourself, to make it seem as though you were also an intended victim—further proof of premeditation. I'll warrant, too, that if you'd had enough time to complete your plan, you would have found a way to frame Lily for the crime. That way, you would have gotten revenge on both of them."

"Sheriff," Lady One-Eye said to Thorpe, "I won't stand for any more of these outrageous accusations. How could I possibly have shot my husband? I was sitting at my table on the platform, in plain sight of the room. My hands were in plain sight, too. If I had drawn a gun and fired it, someone would surely have seen me do it."

"That's right," McFinn said, "*I* would have. I happened to glance at her table before the shot and again just afterward and she was sitting as she said, with her hands in plain sight."

"Yes, she was," Sabina agreed. "I saw her myself. One hand on the table, the other clutching the knob of her cane."

"Well, then?"

"Lady One-Eye is a mistress of sleight of hand. She has been cheating her opponents at poker with the ploy . . . that's right, Mr. McFinn, she *is* a skin-game artist . . . and tonight she used the same principle to dispose of her husband."

"Don't talk in riddles, Mrs. Carpenter. How the devil could she have done it?"

"Remember, there was general confusion at the time; no one was looking closely at her. Remember, too, that the lower half of her body was mostly hidden by the table skirt. And add to those two facts: one, that she was holding her cane, something she never did while she was seated at the poker table; and two, that the lower two-thirds of the cane were out of sight beneath the table skirt."

And in one swift movement Sabina caught hold of the ebony stick, pulled it from Lady One-Eye's grasp, then stepped back with it held out at a horizontal angle. Gaunt lunged forward, but John prevented him from snatching it away from her. She twisted the lion's head knob. The knob was not immovably fastened; rather, it turned on a tight, hidden swivel. One twist slid aside the ferrule on the bottom, and a second twist produced an audible click.

John, who had remained silent throughout Sabina's reconstruction and who was seldom surprised by anything, said a startled, "Hell and damn!"

"Not only a cane," Sabina said, "but a half pistol, half rifle cleverly manufactured of a hollow metal tube disguised as wood and designed to fire a single shot."

7

SABINA

"You've kept me in suspense long enough," John said a short while later, in her room at the Holbrooke. "How did you know Lady One-Eye's cane had been outfitted as a firearm?"

Sabina, freshly bathed, was dressed in one of her own stylishly sedate outfits; the Saint Louis Rose had been packed away in her traveling bag, to be given back to the costumer who had supplied the bawd's various components upon their return to San Francisco. She was tempted to draw out the explanation as John would have, give him a taste of his own medicine, but that would have been petty.

She said, "I once encountered a man in Denver when I was with the Pinkertons who employed a similar device. He had a pegleg that a gunsmith had bored out and fitted with a sawed-off rifle barrel. He fired it through the pocket of his trousers by means of a spring mechanism attached to his thigh."

"Ah. You might have mentioned this to me."

"I had no reason to before tonight. Or to suspect Lady One-Eye's stick of being anything other than what it seemed—not until Jack O'Diamonds was shot and I glimpsed the tip of the cane beneath the table skirt before she pulled it back, saw a faint wisp of smoke rise up at that point."

"And then noticed that her hand was on the knob."

"Yes."

John gnawed on the stem of his favorite briar. He would have liked to smoke it, but she'd forbidden him to do so. The stench of the godawful tobacco he preferred would have been intolerable in the confines of the small room. She really must try to convince him to change his brand.

"It must have taken considerable practice for her to fire her weapon accurately in such a fashion," he said.

"No doubt it did," Sabina agreed. "And no doubt Lady One-Eye carried the weapon for self-protection in the event any of her challengers tumbled to her skin-game tactics, and that she practiced often with it. She may even have had occasion to use the trick a time or two before last night."

"Her brother must have known she was guilty of the murder as soon as it happened. And he'll keep on lying to protect her."

Sabina nodded. "He's fiercely protective, loyal to a fault."

"That, and the fact that she was his meal ticket," John said cynically. "Did you notice how furious he was at you when you revealed her as both a murderer and a card cheat?"

"Oh, yes, I noticed."

"He is a piece of work, and so is she—two of a kind. Her

claim to the sheriff that there was an empty cartridge in the weapon because she'd fired it accidentally this afternoon, and his that he'd witnessed it, are a feeble defense. If it were true, she would surely not have 'forgotten' to reload it. Could the bullet that killed Jack O'Diamonds be matched to the cartridge, she wouldn't have a leg to stand on."

"That's an atrocious pun, John."

"Eh? Oh, strictly unintentional, but nonetheless apt. As it is, there's little doubt that she'll be convicted."

"Don't be too sure. She's bound to use her handicaps to play on the sympathies of a jury. With a certain kind of lawyer representing her, she might succeed in winning an acquittal."

"Not with your eyewitness testimony, and her dubious background."

"We'll see. Juries are notoriously unpredictable."

"Not in conventional mining towns like this one." He gazed fondly at her. "In any case, my dear, I congratulate you. You really are a splendid detective."

"For a woman."

"I didn't say that. Nor did I mean it that way."

"Your equal, then, hmm?"

"Indeed," he said.

Sabina eyed him closely to make sure he was not being condescending. He wasn't. He meant it.

"I'm afraid Mr. McFinn isn't satisfied," she said. "He holds us responsible for not preventing tonight's public spectacle. And with some justification, from his point of view."

"Bah. Even if you'd been certain Lady One-Eye carried a

concealed weapon, it wouldn't have foreshadowed her intent to use it on her husband when and where she did."

"True. But he doesn't see it that way. In a way I feel sorry for him."

"Why? Lady One-Eye's winnings will be confiscated and McFinn reimbursed the two thousand he staked you."

"That doesn't matter to him. What does is that the anti-gambling elements may have enough fuel now to close him down."

John shrugged. "He'd be out of business before long anyway. Small-town gaming parlors such as the Gold Nugget are doomed to extinction."

"You do realize that he might refuse to pay us the balance of our fee?"

His face darkened perceptibly. "By Godfrey, he had better pay it! If he doesn't, we'll add to his woes by bringing suit against him."

Sabina repressed the urge for further comment; when he made up his mind about something, there was no changing it. If it were up to her, she would forfeit the balance of their fee as a gesture of goodwill. From a practical standpoint such largesse could be used as a promotional tool to enhance the reputation of Carpenter and Quincannon, Professional Detective Services. Results guaranteed at no risk to their clients. The new century was almost upon them. Fresh business practices were necessary in a new age.

But she knew better than to suggest this. Like his father and Allan Pinkerton before him, her partner would've been outraged at such a heretical proposition. John Quincannon would rather be horsewhipped than willingly give up a penny earned for services rendered.

Outfitted in her gray serge traveling dress, Sabina was packing the following morning when the knock came at the door. It couldn't be John; he'd gone to see Amos McFee in an effort to collect the remainder of their fee. They had arranged to meet in the Holbrooke's lobby at ten whether he succeeded or not, to first ride to Sheriff Thorpe's office to sign official statements and then to the railroad station to board the NCNG on the first leg of their trip home to San Francisco.

The knock sounded again, more insistent this time. She crossed to open the door. No, it wasn't John. Her caller was Jeffrey Gaunt.

He didn't say anything, merely looked at her. His gray eyes were even colder, more piercing than they had been the previous evening—as palpably cold as the Rocky Mountain high country in winter. But there was a glow of fire in their depths, the fire of hate. The skin between Sabina's shoulder blades crawled; she repressed a shiver.

"What do you want, Mr. Gaunt?"

"I've been told you and your partner are leaving Grass Valley today." His drawling voice was without inflection of any kind.

"There is nothing further to keep us here."

"But you intend to return to testify at my sister's trial."

"Naturally."

"That would be a mistake."

"And why is that?"

"She didn't shoot Jack."

"Of course she did, despite her claims and yours to the contrary. I saw her do it."

"Mistakenly, in a time of turmoil. Or perhaps deliberately to further your own agenda."

"I have no agenda," Sabina said sharply, "except for the pursuit of justice."

"Be that as it may, your unfounded accusations that she is a card mechanic and a murderess have destroyed her reputation and her livelihood. That is reprehensible enough. I won't allow her to be convicted of crimes she didn't commit and sent to prison. Her handicaps would make even a short incarceration a living hell for her."

"Perhaps so, but it's a jury's decision to make, not yours. Or mine."

"I intend to hire the best lawyer in this state to represent her. If you fail to testify, she'll be acquitted and vindicated. I suggest you give that option due consideration."

"Are you threatening me, sir?"

Gaunt said nothing.

"I don't take kindly to threats," Sabina said. "Nor does my partner."

His mouth twitched upward in a brief travesty of a smile.

"Attempting to intimidate a witness in a murder trial is a serious felony, Mr. Gaunt. So, as I shouldn't have to remind you, is any attempted infliction of bodily harm."

"I said nothing about the infliction of bodily harm."

"You implied it. I could have you arrested."

"As you caused my sister to be arrested—on the basis of misinterpretation and enmity. Besides, there is no one else here. It would be your word against mine."

He stared at her a few moments longer, as if trying to will her to show fear or weakness by averting her eyes, and when he received no satisfaction he turned abruptly and walked off down the hall.

She shut and locked the door. He hadn't frightened her in the least; she was far too experienced, strong-willed, courageous to be swayed by threats implied or otherwise. Nevertheless, the afterimage of his frigid eyes and the crawly sensation on her back lingered while she finished her packing.

She waited to tell John of Gaunt's thinly veiled threat until after they were aboard a Southern Pacific passenger train bound from Colfax to Oakland. She knew he'd be furious enough to go storming off to confront the man, and that would have served no purpose except to escalate what might turn out to be a tempest in a teapot.

She said as much to him when he'd calmed down. "We've been threatened before, John, and nothing has come of it. Men like Gaunt are usually nothing more than blowhards."

"Usually, but not always. You saw how fiercely protective he was of his sister last night."

"Yes," Sabina admitted, "I did."

"If you're unable to testify at Lady One-Eye's trial, she may well go free. You were the only witness to her actions after the shooting."

"She could go free even with my testimony," Sabina said. "A handicapped woman is a sympathetic figure, even one with Lady One-Eye's reputation, especially if she's represented by a canny criminal attorney. Gaunt knows that as well as you and I do."

"But we don't know Gaunt, what lurks behind that stoic façade of his, what he's capable of."

"Yes, that's true."

"A man of dark and hidden depths," John said ominously, "that's my estimation of him. A dangerous man. You're to be very careful from now until the trial, my dear."

"I'm always careful, you know that."

"Extra cautious in the city, triple cautious when the time comes for us to return to Grass Valley." He lit his pipe, scowling, and puffed up a great cloud of foul gray smoke. "By God," he muttered, "if that damned rascal comes anywhere near you . . ."

Sabina rested a steadying hand on his arm, smiled when he looked her way. His deep concern touched her. He really did care, not only for her as a partner but as a woman he would do anything in his power to keep safe. If that wasn't love, it was the next thing to it.

8

QUINCANNON

His first order of business the morning after their return to San Francisco was a visit to the Hall of Justice at Portsmouth Square and the office of the only man in the police department he trusted, William Price, head of the Chinatown "flying squad." He had been instrumental the previous year in helping Price avert a deadly tong war and put an end to one element of police corruption, and the lieutenant had been grateful. When he explained what had taken place in Grass Valley, Price agreed to grant him the favor he asked: any information that could be obtained through official channels on the activities of Jeffrey Gaunt and Blanche Gaunt Diamond, aka Lady One-Eye, in California and other western states.

Quincannon's next stop was the Western Union office on Market Street, where he composed and sent two wires. One was to Sheriff Hezekiah Thorpe in Grass Valley, apprising him of Gaunt's threat, asking that he, Quincannon, be notified immediately if Gaunt were to suddenly leave Nevada County. The other wire, marked "Urgent reply requested," was to the Pinkerton Detective Agency's branch office in New Orleans. If Gaunt, Lady One-Eye, and/or Jack O'Diamonds had run afoul of the law in that part of the country, the Pinks would find it out and supply details.

Stop number three was the newsstand of the blind vendor known as Slewfoot, their most reliable informant and information peddler. And number four was Ezra Bluefield's Redemption Saloon on Ellis Street in the Uptown Tenderloin. He had once saved Bluefield's life when the old reprobate owned the Scarlet Lady, a Barbary Coast deadfall, and later helped him realize his desire to purchase the much more respectable Redemption. Quincannon had long since used up his quota of return favors, but this was a special case; he knew he wouldn't be turned away with Sabina's welfare at stake, and he wasn't.

Slewfoot had contacts among the shady characters who operated on the edges of the city's underworld, Bluefield many acquaintances still among the denizens of the Coast. If anyone in San Francisco knew anything about Jeffrey Gaunt and his sister, as problematical as that possibility was, one or both men would ferret it out. Leave no stone unturned.

It was past noon when he entered the offices of Carpenter and Quincannon, Professional Detective Services. Sabina, cool and radiant as always (except when she'd been guised as the Saint Louis Rose), looked up from behind a pile of paperwork on her desk and said, "Well, it's about time, John. Where have you been?"

He told her. "The more we know about Gaunt, the better. He may even be wanted somewhere."

"Possible, but unlikely. You don't intend to keep focusing your energies on him, I trust."

"That depends on what we find out about him."

"If anything other than what little we already know. We've other business to attend to after a five-day absence. Elizabeth received three inquiries from prospective clients during that time."

Elizabeth Petrie, a widowed former police matron and sometime operative when a woman's services were required, had kept the agency open while they were away. She was more than competent. In fact, Sabina had suggested that, considering the amount of work that often kept them both away from the office, hiring Elizabeth as a full-time employee might be a sound idea. The widow, whose only other activity was quilting, and who thrived on detective work, might be amenable to the idea. Quincannon had no objection other than the cost of her salary, but he hadn't voiced this to Sabina; she considered him tight-fisted and money-grubbing enough as it was. (Which was nonsense, of course; he was merely a thrifty Scot.) Besides, they could afford the expense, the more so now that he had badgered Amos McFinn into paying the balance of their fee before they departed Grass Valley.

"What sort of inquiries?" he asked as he shed his coat and derby. The office was warm, as opposed to the day outside, which was overcast and chilly—typical summer weather in San Francisco. The steam radiator made its usual hissing, clanking noises, tolerable enough because it was efficient, but nonetheless distracting at times.

"A routine insurance investigation," Sabina said, "which went to another detective agency when we weren't available. A woman seeking divorce evidence against her philandering husband—Elizabeth told her we don't accept that sort of case. And a wire from a banker in Delford concerning a possible fraud in his community."

"Delford?"

"A small farming town in the San Joaquin Valley."

Quincannon said, "Doesn't sound particularly lucrative, small towns and small-town bankers being what they are."

"That's not necessarily true. And the fraud problem does seem somewhat unusual."

"Yes? What is it?"

"See for yourself. Here's his wire."

Quincannon took it to his desk to read. It was addressed to him, dated the previous day, and had been delivered in the late afternoon.

YOUR AGENCY HIGHLY RECOMMENDED STOP ARRIVING PALACE HOTEL YOUR CITY TUESDAY AFTERNOON STOP REQUEST CONSULTATION REGARDING SUSPECTED PLUVICULTURE FRAUD STOP URGENT STOP KINDLY REPLY STOP
            ARAM KASABIAN
            DELFORD CITIZENS BANK

He laid the wire down, ran fingers through his trimmed whiskers. Sabina liked the beard this way. He wasn't sure he did—he had kept it thick on purpose to project a fierce image to the malefactors he dealt with—but she had implied that it made him even more attractive to her. More than enough reason to keep it in its shortened state.

"Pluviculture," he said. "A fancy word for rainmaking."

"Yes. The San Joaquin Valley is suffering through a severe drought, and Delford's well-being is dependent on sufficient water for wheat and other crops."

"Which makes them a prime target for a rainmaking fraud."

"If it is fraud. Not all pluviculturists are swindlers."

"Most of them are. Disciples of Frank Melbourne, the so-called Australian Rain Wizard."

"We've never handled that type of case before," Sabina said. "Does the prospect appeal to you?"

Quincannon considered. The prospect did in fact hold some appeal. And the Palace Hotel was San Francisco's most luxurious hostelry, which indicated that Aram Kasabian might be a more successful small-town banker than most. But on the other hand . . .

"It's probably not for us," he said.

"No? Why not?"

"It might require a visit to Delford, and we've only just returned from Grass Valley."

"And it might not," Sabina said reasonably. "Besides, back-to-back trips out of town have never bothered you before."

"We'd have to close the agency again."

"Not if you are the only one to go to the San Joaquin Valley."

"And leave you here alone? No."

"Oh, so it's Jeffrey Gaunt you're worried about. John, you can't turn down an investigation because of some nebulous fear for my safety."

"I don't believe it's a nebulous fear."

"I am perfectly capable of taking care of myself and you know it. You act as though I'm a babe in the woods who needs to be watched over twenty-four hours a day."

Quincannon was tempted to say that he would like nothing better than to watch over her twenty-four hours a day. That if he had his druthers she would spend her nights in his flat until the Gaunt concern was resolved. But even if he made such a suggestion, and included a promise that he would sleep on the sofa and make no attempt to seduce her, she would adamantly refuse. And her feathers would be even more ruffled.

He settled for saying, somewhat lamely, "I am only being cautious."

"Overly and unduly cautious. Well, then? *Does* the Delford inquiry interest you?"

"It does," he admitted, "provisionally."

"Then talk to the banker and find out the details. He is already on his way here, so you'll need to contact him at the Palace when he arrives."

"All right. Where's that batch of train schedules?"

"Where it always is, in the second drawer in the file cabinet."

The daily Southern Pacific train from the San Joaquin Valley was due to arrive at the Third and Townsend depot at three o'clock. Given the fact that train timetables were as inaccurate as often as they were accurate—"flexible" was the word the railroad companies used—the actual arrival time might be anywhere from three to four or even later. Transport from the depot to the Palace would take ten to fifteen minutes by cab. No Palace guest, unless he was penurious in the extreme, would care to arrive at a luxury hotel by trolley car. If Aram Kasabian was one of that tightfisted breed, he was not a suitable client.

Several bills, invoices, and requests of one kind and another had piled up during their absence. Quincannon actively hated paperwork and avoided it whenever possible, but he failed to wiggle out of it today. Sabina insisted he help her whittle down the pile and he grumblingly gave in. Until the Seth Thomas on the wall read ten minutes till three, at which time he made haste to depart—just in case, he said to Sabina, the Southern Pacific train defied statistical precedence and arrived on or before schedule.

The Palace, at Third and Market, was a short walk from the agency. A massive, seven-story structure, it had been built in 1875, covered an entire block, and contained more than seven hundred rooms and suites, forty-five public and utility rooms, three inner courts, and an opulently furnished lobby. The time was 3:25 when Quincannon entered. Aram Kasabian had not yet checked in, one of the desk clerks told him. So the good old SP was indeed up to its usual flexible standards today.

He asked the clerk to notify him when the banker arrived, and to tell Mr. Kasabian that John Quincannon was waiting to see him. After which he went to sit in one of the more comfortable of the lobby chairs and tried not to brood about Jeffrey Gaunt while he waited.

9

QUINCANNON

His wait was not a long one. At 3:41 by an ornate lobby clock, a portly middle-aged gent with long bushy side whiskers like miniature tumbleweeds strolled in from the circular Grand Court where carriages and hansoms delivered and picked up guests, and approached the desk. Aram Kasabian? Yes. A bell-boy crossed to where Quincannon sat and confirmed it.

The banker, to Quincannon's practiced eye, appeared to be the prosperous sort. Well and conservatively dressed in a black cheviot suit, starched shirt, and starched collar, his ruddy skin testimony to a liking for rich food and strong spirits. And he was plainly relieved that Quincannon had seen fit to meet him. He said as they shook hands, "I appreciate this, sir, more than I can say. I was afraid when I didn't receive an answer to my wire that I would have to seek out another private investigator."

"My partner and I were out of town on an investigation. We returned only last evening."

"Oh, I see. Yes. Well, I'm certainly glad you did."

Don't be, Quincannon thought, until I decide whether or not your case is worth taking.

He suggested either a corner of the lobby or Kasabian's room for their consultation, but the banker had another suggestion. "I believe I would prefer one of the bar lounges," he said. "After the long train ride, I'm in need of, ah, a small libation while we talk."

They found their way to the nearest of the lounges, settled themselves at a corner table removed from the handful of other patrons. Kasabian's idea of "a small libation" was a double whiskey and soda. Quincannon ordered a glass of plain soda water.

"A temperance man, are you?" Kasabian asked.

"Not at all. I choose not to imbibe for personal reasons."

"Ah, I see. Commendable." His tone of voice indicated that he thought otherwise.

"Is it only the problem mentioned in your wire that has brought you to San Francisco, Mr. Kasabian?"

"Primarily, yes, though I do have other business interests here."

"How long will you be staying?"

"Until Friday. Is that long enough for you to conduct a swift but thorough investigation?"

"That depends on the nature of the suspected pluviculture fraud."

"Yes, of course. I—"

The banker broke off as the uniformed waiter arrived with their drinks. He took a long, deep draught of his whiskey and soda, smacked his lips delicately. Without setting the glass down he reached into the breast pocket of his coat with his free hand and produced a worn leather billfold. From that he extracted an engraved business card, slid it across the table.

LEONIDE DAKS

"THE CLOUD CRACKER"

PEERLESS DROUGHT BREAKING

BY THE KING OF PLUVICULTURISTS

RESULTS GUARANTEED

"Is the name familiar to you, Mr. Quincannon?"

"No."

"Do you believe rain can be induced by man and machine?"

"It would have to be proven to my satisfaction, and it never has been."

"Nor to mine. Or to O. H. Goodland's. But the other members of the Delford Coaltion feel differently—"

Quincannon cut him off with a raised hand. "Not so fast, sir. Who is O. H. Goodland?"

"Yes, I'm getting ahead of myself." The banker took another pull at his drink. "O.H. owns one of the larger wheat farms in our area. He . . . well, he can be rather prickly when he gets his back up. He was against the hiring of this man Daks from the beginning, and has locked horns with him on more than one occasion and for more than one reason."

"And the coalition you mentioned?"

"Other prominent farmers and local businessmen. A dozen, all told. Mr. Goodland and I were outvoted ten to two on the hiring of a 'peerless drought breaker.'"

"How long has Daks been in Delford?"

"A little more than a week."

"Without producing rain."

"Not a drop, not even so much as a cloud. All he has done is assault the heavens and the ears with his infernal device."

"What sort of device?"

"He calls it his 'miracle cloud-cracking machine.' Balderdash."

"How does it operate?"

Kasabian finished his drink and signaled to the waiter for another. Then he explained. Leonide Daks had installed his "infernal machine" in an old watchman's shack at the edge of the Delford railroad yards. Inside, hidden from curious eyes, were what the banker referred to as "a weirdly distorted steam boiler," a variety of chemicals in jars, coils of copper tubing, a galvanic battery, and two large crocks. The combination of items poured streams of yellowish gas into the sky through a tall stovepipe.

But that was but one part of the alleged cloud-cracking machine. Alongside the shack Daks and his assistant, a man named Ben Conley, had constructed a platform that supported another odd contraption, a sort of small, strange-looking cannon. This was used to fire rockets said to contain the "secret chemical gas" manufactured inside the shack. Daks and

Conley had touched off their makeshift cannon several times and planned to continue doing so until the coming weekend.

"He promises at least one-half inch of rain by Saturday evening," Kasabian said, "else he'll admit defeat and return the money the coalition has already paid him."

Quincannon asked how much that was.

"Two thousand dollars. Half the total fee, with the other half to be paid if and when rain is produced."

"And you suspect that unless a natural storm appears, Daks intends to vanish with the money by Friday night."

"Yes. That is what O. H. Goodland and I believe."

"You may well be correct. There have been a number of such frauds perpetrated since the debunking of the practices of Frank Melbourne in 1891."

"Who was he?"

"A confidence man of considerable audacity. He billed himself as the Australian Rain Wizard and bilked thousands of dollars from citizens in Ohio and Wyoming by allegedly 'squeezing rain from cloudless skies as one would squeeze water from a sponge.'"

Quincannon went on to explain that Melbourne had so thrived at first that other opportunists began claiming to have fantastic chemical or electrical machines and formulas of their own devising. Some, such as Clayton B. Jewell and the Kansas-based Inter State Artificial Rain Company, were quasi-legitimate exploiters who utilized Melbourne's trick of consulting long-range almanac forecasts and then gambling on natural storms to follow their cloud-milking folderol. These men operated on a "no rain, no pay" basis. The out-and-out fleecers worked only in communities where drought-weary citizens could be inveigled to pay half their exorbitant fees up front. If no natural storms arrived, allowing them to collect the balance, they were content to disappear with the half already collected.

Kasabian said, "And Leonide Daks is surely another cut from the same cloth. I wish the coalition had known about Melbourne and the rest before they hired him."

"Ignorance and desperation often lead to unwise decisions," Quincannon observed sagely. "How are the other members taking Daks' failure to manufacture rain?"

"There has been some grumbling, but he's a slick-tongued devil. Rainmaking is an inexact art, he says, and it sometimes takes more than a week to produce results. Most of the members and other citizens still have faith in him."

"How exactly did Daks become known to the coalition? By advertisement, or did he simply show up in Delford one day?"

"Advertisement. In the *Sacramento Union*. James Parnell, our mayor, replied and issued an invitation. Daks arrived in a large wagon with his wife, his assistant, and his paraphernalia. Naturally he had all sorts of testimonials to his rainmaking prowess—all of them fake, no doubt. But Mayor Parnell and the others were impressed."

"Where were these testimonials from? What part of the country?"

"Arkansas, Oklahoma, Texas. He had only just moved his operation into the western states and territories, he claimed."

Quincannon considered. Anyone could place a newspaper advertisement; confidence tricksters often did so, in the hope of hooking gullible fish. In Leonide Daks' case, apparently, an entire school of gullible fish. Rainmaking was an elaborate confidence game, requiring such paraphernalia as Kasabian had described, but most of the items—with the possible exception of the cannon—could be had cheaply, abandoned once the marks had been sufficiently milked, and later replaced. Escape from Delford in the middle of the night would not be all that difficult, nor would vanishing to some prearranged hideout before the law could catch them.

He said as much to the banker, who nodded his head between nibbles at his second whiskey and soda. "Can you prevent that from happening, Mr. Quincannon?"

"I can certainly try."

"Then you'll undertake an immediate investigation?"

"If you're in agreement with our standard fee." He named the figure. "Plus any necessary expenses, of course."

Kasabian didn't turn a hair. "Agreed. Mr. Goodland and I will pay it, and gladly, out of our own pockets if our suspicions prove correct."

"Half the fee in advance is customary," Quincannon said, stretching agency policy only slightly.

"A personal check is acceptable, I trust?" At Quincannon's nod, the banker produced a checkbook and proceeded to write.

When Quincannon had the check tucked into his own coat pocket, he said, "Now then. I'll need as much additional information as you're able to provide. A description of Leonide Daks, to begin with."

"Quite tall, thin, with a full beard and a silver-black mane."

"Age?"

"Forty, perhaps a bit younger."

"He has a wife, you said."

"Gloria by name. Fair-haired and quite attractive. In her mid-twenties, I should say. Quite, ah, buxom."

"And the assistant, Conley?"

"A dandy. Several inches shorter than Daks. Sports a thin handlebar mustache and wears his hair slicked down and curled forward above his ears."

Quincannon recorded all of the pertinent information in the little notebook he carried. "One more thing. You stated earlier that O. H. Goodland has locked horns with Daks for more than one reason, his inability to produce rain being one."

"Yes. Mr. Goodland called him a charlatan and worse to his face."

"And the other reason?"

"Mr. Goodland's daughter, Molly. She is young, impressionable. And, well, somewhat smitten with Daks."

"And he with her?"

"Not in the same manner," Kasabian said pointedly.

"As a potential conquest, despite the presence of his wife?"

"Mr. Goodland thinks so. Hence heated warnings to both his daughter and Daks. A potentially volatile situation."

"So it would appear. I take it Mr. Goodland knows you've come to the city to hire a detective?"

"He does, and I have his full backing. How will you conduct your investigation, Mr. Quincannon?"

"A detective never reveals his methods, sir. You'll have to

trust me to do whatever is necessary on your behalf. Satisfactory?"

"Satisfactory. But you will want to travel to Delford—"

"Eventually, perhaps. I'll notify you if so. And of any developments immediately."

He got to his feet; Kasabian rose long enough to shake hands, then sat down again. Quincannon left him peering into his now empty glass as if contemplating the advisability of having it replenished a third time before proceeding to his room.

Quincannon went straight from the Palace to the Miner's Bank on Montgomery Street, where he deposited Aram Kasabian's check. First things first. Then he hied himself once again to the Western Union office a few blocks away.

The first step in a case such as this was the same as that regarding Jeffrey Gaunt, though by different means—to determine just who Leonide Daks (if that was his real name, which likely it wasn't) and his two accomplices were, what sort of criminal records they might have, and whether or not there were any outstanding warrants against them. He composed a semi-coded message containing his requests and the relevant information his client had provided and asking for an ASAP response collect. He had six of them sent, one each to the Pinkerton Agency's branch offices in Chicago, St. Louis, Kansas City, Denver, and Washington, D.C., the last to a private agency in Cincinnati with which Carpenter and Quincannon, Professional Detective Services, had done business in the past. Given the length of the wires, the charges were substantial. Not that this mattered, of course. He made a note of the total amount, to be added, along with the collect reply fees, to the Kasabian expense account.

Sabina was just finishing up the last of the paperwork when he returned to the agency. Had there been any further word from William Price regarding Jeffrey Gaunt? he asked her. Or from Slewfoot or Ezra Bluefield? No, nothing as yet. She told him not to be impatient, it was too soon to expect results, and of course she was right.

He filled her in on his meeting with the Delford banker and the probable rainmaking fraud. "It's just the sort of investigation you thrive on," she said when he finished. "A trip to Delford certainly seems indicated."

"Perhaps. It depends on the answers to the wires I sent."

He asked her if she would mind transcribing his notes into a case file. She told him a bit snippily to do it himself, it was his case. This was the answer he'd expected, and the proper one, but his dislike of paperwork had led him to ask. Every now and then, if she were in the right mood, she would accommodate him.

When he finished preparing the file, it was nearly five o'clock. He set down his pen, tapped dottle from his pipe into the desk ashtray. "Will you have dinner with me tonight, my dear?" he asked. "I thought perhaps the Old Poodle Dog—"

"No, not tonight. I have things to attend to."

"What things?"

"Errands. Personal matters. Don't be so inquisitive."

"At least let me see you home—"

"For heaven's sake, John, you're as transparent as glass.

How many times do I have to tell you I'm perfectly capable of taking care of myself?"

It was on the tip of his tongue to say he couldn't help worrying about her, he wanted her to be safe, he . . . well, dammit, he *cared* for her. But he couldn't get the words out, and it was just as well he couldn't. It would have embarrassed him, because he knew he was being overprotective and because he was not ready to declare himself. Soon, mayhap, but not yet. Not yet.

10

She spent a quiet, relaxing evening with Adam and Eve.

After yesterday's train trips from Grass Valley to Oakland, the ferry ride across the bay, and a rattling cab ride to her apartment building, she'd been too weary to pay much attention to the two cats; she had gone straight to bed. Today had been long and tiring, too, what with returning the Saint Louis Rose outfits to the costumers, all the catch-up work at the office, and some necessary shopping on the way home. She needed time to herself, away from John and his well-meaning but overbearing concern, and then a more restful night's sleep.

Eve, an Abyssinian female, had taken to Adam from the moment Charles the Third gifted her with the coal-black male, then just a kitten, at the close of the Body Snatchers Affair last year. A maternal streak on Eve's part, perhaps. The two cats were good company for each other, comported well together, but they craved Sabina's affection. They followed her around the apartment, curled up on her lap when she sat in her morris chair and next to her in bed, even gazed at her with watchful, wondering eyes while she treated herself to a soak in the copper-lined, bronze-legged tub in her bathroom.

The apartment was comfortable enough—four rooms in an older building near the foot of Russian Hill—but John's quarters were much more spacious. She'd been surprised at its size on that one recent visit, a five-room flat that was certainly large enough for two. If he ever did propose to her, and if she accepted (the jury was likely to remain out on both for some time), he would surely want her to move in with him. Would she be content to share what was clearly a masculine abode designed for seduction as well as comfort? For a while, perhaps, but only if he first agreed to replace the hideous gold-framed mirror decorated with nude nymphs in his parlor. And agreed to eventually seek out new and different quarters that suited them both . . .

Oh, for heaven's sake, Sabina, she chided herself, *what's the matter with you? You're getting way ahead of yourself. Stop acting like a lovesick prospective bride.*

Besides, she was quite content living here with Adam and Eve. Well? Wasn't she?

She stepped out of the tub, toweled herself vigorously with some playful and unwanted assistance from Adam. Before she put on her dressing gown, the bathroom mirror gave her a glimpse of her nakedness. Her body was still as lissome as it had been when she was a girl, her breasts still high, still firm. Looking at them, she remembered the touch of Stephen's caressing hands. He was the only man who had ever caressed her in that intimate fashion, and it had been more than five years now since the bandit's bullet had destroyed his life and theirs together. For a long time afterward she neither wanted intimacy with anyone else nor even thought about it. But lately, at moments in John's company, she'd felt stirrings of the passion that Stephen had kindled in her. Even had not one but two erotic dreams about John, the second quite vivid, that still brought color to her face whenever she thought about them. Would his touch, his caresses arouse her as Stephen's had? Would he be as gentle and expert a lover—?

She felt her face grow warm, quickly covered herself with the robe. Perhaps she *was* a bit lovesick after all. And she didn't want to be, confound it. Not now!

In the parlor, she was drawn to the framed photograph of Stephen on the mantelpiece. Such a handsome man, slender, his high-browed head topped with a wealth of black curls. She looked upon his image, as she often did, with deep sadness. He had been the love of her life; no man could ever take his place in her heart. But he would not have wanted her to go on mourning him for the rest of her life, to deny herself the happiness and pleasure of another relationship. He had said as much to her once, when they first moved from Chicago to Denver to join the Pinkerton Agency's office there—that if anything should happen to him, she must remain strong and move on with her life.

She wondered, not for the first time, how he would have felt about John. Would he have approved of John's sometimes unorthodox and idiosyncratic methods, his sly sense of humor, his lofty opinion of his detective abilities? Would they have gotten along had they ever met? She sensed that they would have. They were cut from the same cloth, both courageous, strong-willed, dedicated, compassionate, caring. Stephen would have admired John, and John him, she decided. The thought was somehow comforting.

In the small kitchen and dining room, Sabina gave the cats another portion of the raw fish they liked and then prepared a light supper for herself. Finished eating, she sat in the parlor with a copy of *The Old Curiosity Shop*. Dickens was one of her favorites; she found his work both stimulating and relaxing, the kind of fiction in which she could lose herself for hours at a time. She read until after ten o'clock, and when she went to bed Adam and Eve followed her and curled up at her side.

She dreamed of Stephen, a dream the details of which she couldn't remember in the morning. But John was in it, too, lurking . . . no, that was the wrong word . . . hovering somewhere in the background. . . .

The first responses to her partner's various inquiries were delivered shortly after she opened the office for business on Thursday morning. One was a wire from the Pinkerton office in Kansas City, stating that they had no information on the self-styled "cloud cracker" who called himself Leonide Daks. The second came by telephone from police lieutenant William Price, shortly after John arrived; he took the call. From his end of the conversation, and his frustrated expression when he ended it, Sabina knew what to expect even before he spoke to her.

"Not a blasted thing on Jeffrey Gaunt," he said. "No known criminal record in California, Arizona, or Nevada."

"Lady One-Eye? Her late husband?"

"The same. You spotted her card manipulation trick, but no one else seems to have since her arrival in this part of the country." He added darkly, "Or to have survived long enough to press charges if they did."

"She is, or was, a very good mechanic," Sabina said. "And very careful to use her trick only when it gave her a definite advantage. No one else she played was privy to my knowledge or experience, evidently."

"At least not in three states. But Price agreed to check with others. And mayhap the Pinkerton office in New Orleans will have news when they respond to my wire."

In the next hour two more collect wires were delivered in tandem by a Western Union messenger. One was from the Pinkerton office in Denver, signed by a resident operative Sabina knew from her Pink Rose days, Jeremy Link; the other was from the detective agency in Cincinnati. Neither had a dossier on a bogus rainmaker answering to the descriptions and methodology of Leonide Daks and his cohorts.

The lack of progress put John into one of his restless funks. He left shortly afterward on an unspecified errand, saying he would return in the early afternoon.

Not long after his departure, a second call came through the Telephone Exchange. This one was for Sabina, from her cousin, Callie French.

Callie was not only her closest living relative, but her best friend in the city. Like Sabina, Callie had been born in

Chicago, but her family had moved to California five years later, lived in Oakland for a time, then settled in San Francisco when her father was promoted to the regional headquarters of the Miner's Bank. Shortly after her debut as a debutante, she had married Hugh French, a protégé of her father's, in a lavish wedding that reputedly (though incorrectly, as Callie later confided) cost fifty thousand dollars. When Sabina had come here from Denver to join John in establishing Carpenter and Quincannon, Professional Detective Services, Callie had been her entrée into the lives and intrigues of the city's social elite.

As kind and supportive as she was, she had two less than endearing traits. One was that of inveterate matchmaker, having been the catalyst for Sabina's brief and abortive romance with Carson Montgomery the previous year, and since then a staunch promoter of her budding personal relationship with John. The other was constant fretting over the dangers of Sabina's profession. It was the latter that had prompted her call.

"Oh, I'm so glad you're back safe and sound," her voice said in relieved tones. "You know how I worry when I don't hear from you. Did everything go well in . . . where was it you and John went? Nevada County?"

"Yes. Our investigation had a satisfactory resolution."

"I would love to hear the details, if you're able to confide them."

"Well, some, perhaps."

"And I have some juicy bits of gossip to share with you in return," Callie said. "Are you free for luncheon today, dear?"

Sabina hesitated, but only for a moment. She had to eat,

after all; and there was little enough for her to do here at the moment. Callie was always pleasant company and her tidbits of gossip worth listening to, and she wouldn't be put off a get-together for long. Today was as good a time as any.

They arranged to meet at noon at the Sun Dial, one of Callie's favorite restaurants. As usual, her cousin was already at table when Sabina arrived, her plump and tightly corseted body encased in a stylish Charvet dress and chemisette, her blond hair braided and coiled in the current fashion. Past her fiftieth year now, she was still a handsome woman, though her fondness for sweets had added some twenty pounds to her once svelte figure.

Callie was full of questions as they dined, she on a veal chop, Sabina on crab cakes. She chuckled at Sabina's account of her make-believe performance as the Saint Louis Rose, exclaimed over the turn of events that had led to the fatal shooting of Jack O'Diamonds, expressed astonishment at the method with which Lady One-Eye had disposed of her philandering husband.

The one thing Sabina made no mention of was Jeffrey Gaunt's threat; it would have thrown Callie into a tizzy of concern greater than John's, led her once again to fuss over the dangers, real and imagined, of Sabina's profession.

Her "juicy bits of gossip" in return were of the mildly scandalous variety. One of her very best friends—she had the grace not to name the woman—was indulging in a clandestine affair with a tradesman well below her station. And a business acquaintance of Hugh's, whom Callie did name, had made a series of bad investments and was in serious financial straits as a result. Prattle, for the most part, to which Sabina listened politely. Transgression among the upper echelons of society held little interest for her unless they had relevance within her own sphere—as had been the case earlier in the year when the life of her suffragist friend Amity Wellman had been endangered as the result of a foolish *affaire de coeur*.

Over dessert, Callie probed, as she was wont to do, into Sabina's personal life. Had John shown any inclination that he was thinking of asking for her hand in marriage? No? Oh, but he would, surely. And the answer would be yes when he did, wouldn't it? Callie's eyes gleamed eagerly; there was nothing she'd have liked better than to arrange and host a lavish wedding celebration along the lines of her own. Sabina would have liked nothing less. Pomp and circumstance of any kind held no appeal for her. If John ever did propose and she accepted, their union would be a small, quiet, and dignified event, no matter how much Callie protested.

It was one-forty when they parted company, and nearly two when Sabina returned to the agency. As she was about to enter the building, a voice called her name. She turned to see the familiar Western Union messenger, a lad named Silas, hurrying toward her with an envelope in hand.

"Another collect wire, Mrs. Carpenter," he said. "You folks sure must be busy these days. This is the fifth I've delivered today and the second in the past hour."

"Yes, very busy. How much is it?"

"Twelve seventy-five. Another long one. Even longer than the previous one—that was eleven-twenty. For a change Mr. Quincannon didn't bat an eye when he paid me." A reference to John's usual grumbling manner whenever he was required to pay cash for something that could not be added to a client's expense account.

"I don't have that much in my bag," Sabina said. "Come upstairs and I'll pay you in the office."

"Yes, ma'am. Gladly."

The agency door was locked; John had gone again after receiving the other long wire. Inside, she took thirteen dollars from petty cash and paid Silas, telling him to keep the quarter change for himself. It would make up for the lack of any largesse from John on the previous delivery. Naturally he didn't believe in tipping for services rendered.

His desktop was empty, as was hers; he must have taken the other wire with him. Something to do with the Delford matter, then. If it contained information regarding Jeffrey Gaunt, he would have remained here to show it to her or left it for her to peruse.

The newly delivered wire had been sent by the agent in charge of the Pinkerton's New Orleans office. And it *did* contain information on Blanche Gaunt Diamond and her brother.

The semi-coded message translated to this: Although neither Jeffrey Gaunt nor his sister had a criminal record in Louisiana or Texas, they had been suspected of criminal acts in both states. Lady One-Eye of cheating at cards, Gaunt of being mixed up in a shady land-speculation deal with a man named D. S. Nickerson—and both of involvement in not one but two homicides.

The first of the homicides had taken place in New Orleans

five years ago, shortly after the land-speculation swindle was uncovered. A small-time gambler named Purdy had publicly accused Lady One-Eye of fleecing him at poker; she had denied the charge and her brother had threatened Purdy in front of witnesses. Three days later the gambler had been shot to death in a crowded French Quarter club—Lady One-Eye perhaps having been responsible, by means of the same hidden-revolver trick she'd used to dispatch her philandering husband. She and Gaunt were questioned by police and released for lack of evidence, but both were ordered to leave New Orleans and never return. Jack O'Diamonds was not involved, having been away on one of the Mississippi River packets at the time.

The victim in the second homicide, three years ago in San Antonio, had been a wealthy landowner, Herman Jackson, who'd taken a shine to Lady One-Eye and made bold advances to her. No public threats were made against him by either her or her brother, but not long afterward he had been found dead in a horse stall in his stable, his head bashed in. Again Gaunt and Lady One-Eye had been questioned but not charged. For lack of evidence to the contrary, a coroner's jury had concluded that the landowner had been kicked to death by one of his prize thoroughbreds.

As provocative as this material was, it provided no proof that Jeffrey Gaunt had gone to lethal lengths to protect and avenge his sister. He may have killed the Texas landowner, and been complicit in the murder of the New Orleans gambler, but it was also possible that neither of them had had a hand in the first death and that the second had in fact been accidental.

John would surely take the grim view, that of Gaunt as a cold-blooded murderer, and insist upon acting as her bodyguard until after Lady One-Eye's trial, to the neglect of the Delford matter and his other investigative work. It might even incite him to rush back to Grass Valley and confront Gaunt—a foolish act with potentially deadly consequences.

She couldn't let either of those things happen. And since he might not listen to the voice of reason, there was only one way to prevent it.

Don't let him see the wire.

Sabina refolded it, returned it to the envelope, and tucked the envelope into the bottom drawer of her desk. Withholding pertinent information from her partner was something she seldom did, but in this case it seemed justified. She was not afraid of Jeffrey Gaunt, whether he was murderously inclined or not, and she refused to be intimidated or coddled.

Let him attempt to carry out his threat; he would regret it if he did. She was as adept with pistol or derringer as any man alive.

11

QUINCANNON

The daily train to Stockton and the San Joaquin Valley departed from Third and Townsend at 9:45 A.M. Aram Kasabian had already boarded and was waiting in the private Pullman compartment he'd booked when Quincannon arrived. The banker was still plainly nervous, his hands opening and closing restlessly as if he were attempting to pluck dust mites from the pale shaft of sunlight filtering in through the window.

Quincannon stowed his valise on the overhead rack. It was still cool in the city, but he wore a lightweight linen suit and blue silk vest in anticipation of the San Joaquin Valley heat. Kasabian, on the other hand, was once again draped in his banker's duds, the starched collar included.

"I hope there won't be any delays today," he said as Quincannon took the seat across from him. "The sooner we arrive in Delford, the better for my nerves."

"Fretting won't get us there any more quickly."

"I know. But I can't help worrying that Daks—"

"Saxe," Quincannon corrected. "Leopold Saxe."

"Yes, that Saxe and his accomplices have already absconded with the coalition's payment."

"They have no cause to believe that we're onto them, or that they're about to be arrested."

"They still might have decided to leave early."

"If they did, our wire yesterday to your town marshal will have prevented it. You said Tom Boxhardt is a competent lawman."

"Yes, but with no experience in this sort of business. His peacekeeping duties are mostly limited to the arrest of drunks and rowdies on Saturday night. He also has but one deputy."

"And the authority, don't forget, to deputize others if necessary."

Kasabian mopped his forehead dry with a large red handkerchief. "I would feel better if he had the authority to arrest the lot of them."

"But he doesn't, not without a proper warrant. Technically the con artists have yet to do anything illegal in Delford."

"But they're wanted in two states—"

"Three."

"All the more reason for them to be held until County Sheriff Beadle arrives from Fresno with the warrant. I still don't see why the wire you received wasn't sufficient cause for Marshal Boxhardt to take them into custody."

Quincannon reined in a sharp retort. The wire, now safely tucked into the breast pocket of his coat, had come from an operative named Hooper in the Pinkerton Agency's Chicago office. Hooper had provisionally identified "Leonide Daks" as an alias of Leopold Saxe, and his two cohorts as Mortimer Rollins and Cora Lee Johnson. Saxe and Rollins had operated confidence swindles dating back ten years, to their days as Chicago theatrical performers—low comedy and specialty acts in variety beer halls. More confidence men than one might suppose had such backgrounds. Since becoming professional con artists they had left a trail of victims in Illinois, Missouri, and Nebraska. Rainmaking was their most recent dodge, begun when Saxe had met and taken up with Cora Lee Johnson in Omaha two years ago; she was his mistress, not his wife. Before that the men had posed as mining-stock speculators, purveyors of a fountain-of-youth elixir, and inventors of an electric cancer cure.

With more patience than he felt Quincannon once again pointed out to his client that the wire and the information it contained held no legal weight; that despite the similarity in names Leonide Daks had not yet been officially identified as Leopold Saxe, nor his accomplices under their real names.

"But if their true identities haven't been verified," Kasabian said, "how could the arrest warrant have been issued?"

Quincannon refrained from asking him how a seemingly intelligent banker could be so dull-witted on occasion. He and Hooper had notified the authorities in the three states where Saxe, Rollins, and Cora Lee Johnson were wanted, and of their suspicions that the threesome was presently operating in northern California; this had been enough for the Illinois attorney general to request that they be arrested and detained.

Once their identities were confirmed, extradition would be arranged.

He had just finished explaining this for the second time when the engineer sounded his whistle and the conductor's shout of "All aboard!" went up. Kasabian heaved a long sigh as the cars jerked into motion. "About time," he said.

Quincannon produced, charged, and fired his pipe. The banker continued to fidget as the train rolled out of the yards, began to pick up speed. "I must say, Mr. Quincannon," he said then, "I'm glad you consented to join me today. It's not a trip I would have relished taking alone."

"I always see my investigations through to the finish."

"Commendable, sir. Commendable."

Such had been Quincannon's code of ethics throughout his careers as Secret Service operative and private investigator, and he had never yet broken it. But he was reluctant nonetheless in this case. Neither his wires, Lieutenant Price's inquiries, nor the efforts of Ezra Bluefield and Slewfoot had produced a single bit of information about Jeffrey Gaunt. Or, for that matter, Lady One-Eye. This should have eased his concern over Sabina's safety, but it didn't.

She'd insisted that he make the trip. As she rightly pointed out, his usual stellar detective work was responsible for the apprehension of three wanted fugitives, and it was fitting and proper that he be present to receive the accolades of Delford's citizens and the county law. Well and good, then. If all went according to plan, he would be back in San Francisco tomorrow afternoon. A day and a half was not such a long time to be away, after all—or so he kept telling himself.

The ride to Delford seemed interminable, the more so because Kasabian in his nervousness indulged in nonstop chatter even when Quincannon pretended to be asleep. And once they entered the San Joaquin Valley, the intense summer heat turned the compartment into a sweatbox. Opening a window was not an option; it would only have let in flying cinders from the locomotive's stacks as well as more dry heat.

A noonday meal in the dining car helped pass some of the time. Afterward Quincannon sought to escape the banker's company by entering the club car, but Kasabian followed him and proceeded to down two large whiskies and soda, the liquor serving to make him more talkative. By the time they reached the farming community in mid-afternoon, Quincannon's patience and temper were both on short leashes.

The old watchman's shack Leopold Saxe had made his headquarters was at the south end of the railroad yards, a short distance from the station. As the train passed it, slowing and hissing steam, he had a clear look at it. And at a portion of the field behind it where the swindlers' equipage—a roan horse and what looked to be a converted dougherty wagon—were picketed.

The shack was a ramshackle affair, listing a few degrees farther south on one side, its dusty windows blinded by squares of monk's cloth. Half a dozen citizens lounged in the shade of a small copse of locust trees at the rim of the field nearby—far fewer, no doubt, than had been in attendance when Saxe began his rain-conjuring experiments the previous week.

The length of brand-new stovepipe that poked up more than a dozen feet through the shack's roof was presently emitting clouds of the yellowish gas Kasabian had described. The contraption on the wooden platform that had been erected alongside resembled a cross between a cannon and a gigantic slingshot. Stretched between the platform and the building was a silken banner festooned with ribbons that hung limp in the hot dry air. The crimson words emblazoned on the banner were the same as those on the Cloud Cracker's business card.

When the train stopped in the station, Quincannon and Kasabian were the only two passengers to alight. Of course not a trace of cloud, cracked or otherwise, marred the smoky blue of the sky overhead. Nor was there even the faintest whiff of ozone among the mingled odors of summer dust, river water, and the noxious chemical gas. Quincannon thought sourly that the temperature here must be at least ten degrees higher than it had been in Grass Valley, the faint breeze like a breath from an open furnace. Sweat immediately slicked his face, trickled through the hairs of his beard as he stood surveying the town of Delford.

It stretched out to the north and east, some five square blocks in size, its main street defined by orderly rows of gaslight standards, electricity not having come into general use here as yet, and zinc-sheathed telegraph poles. The few crop, hay, and freight wagons that moved along it raised puffs and spurts of dust that seemed to hang suspended in the lifeless air. There was hardly any pedestrian activity, owing to the heat and the fact that this was a farm community still caught in the vise of a drought. Wheat fields surrounded it, broken only by the Southern Pacific tracks on one side and the willow-lined banks of the San Joaquin River on the other.

Two men who had been standing in the shade of the depot's roof stepped out together and came forward. Both were middle-aged, one very fat and bald except for little sprouts of gray hair here and there on his scalp, the other thin and lantern-jawed. Kasabian introduced the fat man as James Parnell, mercantile proprietor and mayor of Delford, and the thin gent as town marshal Tom Boxhardt. Quincannon hardly needed the introduction to deduce Boxhardt's occupation; a badge was pinned to his shirt under a sweat-stained cowhide vest, and he wore an old-fashioned Civil War–vintage Beaumont-Adams revolver in a side holster. Parnell's handshake was moist, Boxhardt's firm and dry.

The banker looked around nervously before saying, "Sheriff Beadle and his deputies haven't arrived yet, I take it."

"Not yet," Parnell said. He had a high, reedy voice, incongruous in a man of his bulk. A gleaming watch chain a quarter of an inch thick bisected his bulging corporation. "No, not yet."

Just as well, Quincannon thought. The sheriff's tardy arrival would allow him to join in the arrest of the three swindlers.

"When are they coming?" Kasabian asked Boxhardt. "Have you had word?"

"No. Better be soon, though. Matters have heated up, and I don't mean the weather."

"Those crooks haven't tried to leave?"

"No. They're still at work in the shack. Fired off them

chemical bombshells of theirs the last two nights and claim they'll do the same again tonight."

"Then what—?"

"Trouble between Daks and Mr. Goodland."

"What kind of trouble? What's happened?"

"O.H. threatened to kill the rainmaker last evening."

"Oh Lord. For what reason?"

"Evidently Daks, or Saxe, made improper advances to his daughter," Parnell said distastefully. "May even have seduced the poor girl. Molly denied it, but Mr. Goodland's not convinced."

Quincannon asked when and where the advances were made.

"Same day Mr. Kasabian left for San Francisco, over in the willow grove by the river. The girl went there for the evening shade and Saxe followed her. Mr. Goodland found out yesterday afternoon, when he came upon Molly crying in her room."

"Does Saxe's mistress know about this?"

"Well, she wasn't there when he accosted Daks, but she must've heard by now. The other one . . . Rollins, is it? . . . was there when it happened outside the Valley House."

"Accosted?" Kasabian said. He was putting his red handkerchief to use again, mopping his ruddy cheeks and neck inside the already wilted starched collar. "Were blows struck?"

"Worse'n that," Boxhardt said. He spat into the dust beyond the edge of the station platform. "Mr. Goodland was carrying his revolver and he drew the weapon when the rainmaker give him no satisfaction. I disarmed him, warned him against any more violence. But you know how he is."

"All too well. Stubborn, and a grudge-holder. There's no telling what he might do."

Quincannon asked, "Is he here in town today?"

"Never left," Boxhardt said. "Took a room last night at the hotel, down the hall from Saxe's and the woman's room."

"Any more trouble between them since?"

"Not that I know about."

"Is he at the hotel now?"

"In the saloon, last I saw of him."

"Building his courage with whiskey," Kasabian said. His disapproving tone was wryly ironic, given his own penchant for strong spirits. "O.H. is temperamental enough when he's sober, but under the influence he is twice as unpredictable."

"He hasn't been told about the fugitive arrest warrant?"

Mayor Parnell said, "No, of course not. No one in town knows but the four of us."

Quincannon leaned down to pick up his valise. "Suppose we go have a talk with Mr. Goodland," he said, "and make sure he keeps a tight rein on his temper until Sheriff Beadle arrives."

12

QUINCANNON

The Valley House was a plain, two-story frame building opposite the bank. It had two entrances, one marked HOTEL and the
other GENTLEMEN'S SALOON. When Quincannon followed Kasabian, Boxhardt, and Parnell through the latter, he found himself
in a dim, stuffy room ripe with the smells of beer and spirits. A
handful of patrons were lined along the bar and two old men
played cribbage at one of the tables.

"O.H. isn't here," the banker said. "Perhaps he went up to
his room—"

Loud, angry voices from the adjacent lobby interrupted
him. One, a tolerable bellow, prompted Boxhardt to say,
"That's Mr. Goodland." He hurried through the archway sep-
arating the saloon from the lobby.

At the foot of the staircase to the upper floor, a burly gent
in farmer's garb stood nose to nose with a slender young man
in a cutaway coat and brocade vest. A flaxen-haired woman

clad in a white shirtwaist and flowered skirt was making an effort to push the farmer, no doubt O. H. Goodland, away. He took no notice; she might have been pushing at a rooted tree.

". . . all of you out of town before noon tomorrow," Goodland was shouting, "or you'll suffer the consequences." The words carried a whiskey slur. Veins stood out on his thick neck; his sunburned face had darkened apoplectically. "You hear me, Conley? You and Daks and this woman here and all your damned paraphernalia by noon tomorrow!"

Mortimer Rollins, alias Ben Conley, was four inches shorter and fifty pounds lighter, but he, too, stood his ground. Flashing eyes and the hard set of his mouth belied the dandified appearance given him by the thin handlebar mustache and sleekly pomaded hair. He was neither afraid of the farmer nor intimidated by him.

"Your threats are worthless, sir," he said. "We intend to remain in Delford until we have fulfilled our contract to bring rain to this parched land—"

"Rain! Humbug! Not a cloud much less a cloudburst in six days."

"We are scientists, not wizards."

Goodland uttered a rude word that brought a gasp from the woman and a "Here now!" protest from the mayor. Quincannon thought the gasp was theatrical; Cora Lee Johnson had likely heard—and spoken—far worse in her twenty-eight years. She was small and soft-looking, but there would be sand and cold steel at the core of her.

She said with spirit, "You are vulgar, sir, as well as a drunkard and a fool."

"Better a vulgar fool than a charlatan and a debaucher."

"My husband is not a charlatan. And he did not seduce your daughter."

"Can't deny he made advances to her."

"I can and I do deny it."

"By God, she told me he did and she's not a liar."

"Then she must have imagined or misinterpreted the situation. Now will you kindly allow us to proceed to our rooms?"

"Proceed to the devil, the lot of you," Goodland snapped. "You'll be welcomed with open arms."

At this insult Rollins' control deserted him. He launched a blow without warning, one that, despite his small stature, had a good deal of force behind it when it landed on the farmer's chin. Goodland reeled backward and went down, but only for the length of time it took him to shake his head and roar out a savage oath; then he scrambled to his feet with his fists cocked. He would have charged Rollins if Quincannon hadn't moved in quickly to grab hold of him, pin his arms at his sides.

Goodland struggled, and when he couldn't break loose he swiveled his head to see who had him in such an iron grip. "Who the hell are you?" he demanded.

Kasabian said quickly, "He's the, ah, the man I went to San Francisco to see. John Quincannon."

"Yeah? Well, let go of me."

"Not until you agree to behave," Boxhardt told him.

"That damned fop hit me—"

"You seem to've given him good reason."

Goodland repeated the rude word, tried again to pull free.

"You've had a bit too much to drink and it's an infernally hot day," Quincannon said. "A bad combination, sir."

He applied pressure on the farmer's right arm until Goodland grunted and subsided. "All right, blast you. You needn't break my arm."

Quincannon, with Boxhardt's assistance, led him to a nearby wing chair and bent him into it. Goodland stayed put, massaging his arm and muttering to himself.

Leopold Saxe's mistress said, "You have our gratitude, Mr. . . . Quincannon, is it?"

He essayed a slight bow. "Yes. An acquaintance of Mr. Kasabian's."

She introduced herself as Nora Daks and Rollins under his assumed name. "What brings you to Delford, if I may ask?"

"I am a reporter with the *Call-Bulletin*," Quincannon lied glibly, "come to witness the marvels of pluviculture firsthand. I had hoped to arrive earlier in the week, but another matter kept me in the city. I seem not to have missed either a deluge or a sprinkle thus far."

"You'll see the latter shortly," Rollins said.

"Indeed? And the former?"

"By Saturday morning at the latest. Given sufficient time, the Cloud Cracker's miracle formula always produces the desired results."

"Always? In every venue?"

"Absolutely. Guaranteed."

"I look forward to meeting the great man."

"He'll want to meet you, too," Cora Lee said. "Come to the

rail yards before seven this evening and Mr. Conley and I will arrange for an introduction and an interview."

"He'll be bruising the sky again with his rockets this evening?"

"Yes. Promptly at seven."

When she and Rollins had gone upstairs, Quincannon and Boxhardt wasted no time in hoisting O. H. Goodland out of the wing chair and marching him past a wide-eyed desk clerk and out through the hotel's rear door. The wheat farmer's protests were mild; heat, exertion, and alcohol had combined to make him both sluggish and docile. Kasabian and Parnell trailed along behind.

In the shade of the hotel livery barn Quincannon sat Goodland down again on a bale of hay. A water pump and trough beckoned nearby. Neither the marshal nor the two businessmen objected when he pumped up half a dipperful and doused the farmer's head. This roused Goodland, brought him sputtering to his feet.

"How dare you! You . . . you . . ."

"Are you sober enough now to listen to reason?"

"Mr. Quincannon and I have news, O.H.," Kasabian told him hastily. "News you'll be glad to hear."

"That scoundrel's death is the only news that would cheer me." Goodland pushed up off the hay bale, dried his face with the sleeve of his shirt. His spurt of anger seemed to dry with it. He regarded Quincannon through eyes that were bleary but focused. "You're a detective, eh. Well? What's your news?"

Succinctly Quincannon told him who and what the Cloud

Cracker and his cohorts were, and of the arrest warrant and the imminent arrival of Sheriff Beadle and his two deputies to take the trio into custody. The news put a small, satisfied smile on Goodland's mouth and a gleam in his bloodshot eyes.

"Frauds and highbinders," he said. "By Christ, I knew it all along. How'd you find all this out so quick?"

"Detective work of the most advanced and perspicacious sort. Did you think Mr. Kasabian would hire a commonplace detective, sir?"

"No, no, not at all. I had faith in Aram's judgment."

Quincannon fixed him with a steely eye. "Now that you know what to expect, I trust you won't attempt to confront the miscreants again."

"Put your mind at rest, sir. Now that I know Daks or Saxe or whatever the scoundrel's name is headed for prison, I'll not try to avenge my daughter's honor."

"You'll return to your farm, then?"

"No, that I won't do. Not until I see him arrested with my own eyes." Goodland paused, frowning. "Why haven't Beadle and his deputies shown up by now? What's keeping them?"

"They'll be along soon," Boxhardt said.

"They'd better be." Goodland added his favorite rude word and stalked back into the hotel.

But Beadle and his deputies didn't arrive soon. And wouldn't today or tonight.

It was while Quincannon sat sweltering with Boxhardt in

the marshal's cramped, bakery-oven office at the jail that the town's telegrapher delivered the wire. He read it over Boxhardt's shoulder.

ARRIVAL UNAVOIDABLY DELAYED UNTIL NOON TOMORROW EARLIEST STOP REGRET ADDITIONAL DELAY POSSIBLE WILL NOTIFY IN THAT EVENT STOP

A BEADLE

"Regret additional delay possible" might mean late Friday or Saturday before Beadle and his deputies finally showed up. The prospect scratched at Quincannon's temper like a thorn. The longer the delay, the shorter the odds that O. H. Goodland would lose his head once he found out, or that Saxe, Rollins, and Cora Lee would attempt to abscond with the coalition's two thousand dollars. Not only that, but the delay also meant that he was stuck here for one, two, possibly even three more days.

At the Valley House, Quincannon booked a room, staying in its cauldronlike atmosphere just long enough to deposit his valise and douse his face and hands from the jug of tepid water provided by the establishment. Boxhardt had gone to inform Aram Kasabian and James Parnell at their places of business of the delay. O. H. Goodland had not been informed, nor would he be. There had been no sign of him since the conversation earlier. Ensconced in his room, if he had any sense; if he'd foolishly decided to do any more imbibing, it was somewhere other than in the hotel bar.

Quincannon was sitting in a wing chair in a corner of the lobby, pretending to read a two-day-old copy of the Stockton *Record,* when Cora Lee Johnson came downstairs. She was alone, Rollins having left twenty minutes earlier and the as yet unseen Leopold Saxe evidently still at the watchman's shack. He watched her walk across the lobby and pass outside. On her way to an early supper, he judged, before joining her comrades for yet another spurious rocket assault.

He consulted his Hampden pocket watch; the time was ten before six. He laid the paper aside, climbed the stairs to the second floor. He had learned from the desk clerk which rooms were occupied by Saxe and Cora Lee and by Rollins; Rollins' was closest and he went there first. The door was locked, of course, but this presented little difficulty to a man of Quincannon's talents. The handy little set of burglar tools he carried in his pocket gave him access in less than a minute.

A thorough search of luggage, furnishings, and other possible hiding places turned up no hint of the Delford Coalition's two thousand dollars. Finding and confiscating the cash would not only ensure that the coalition was repaid, but help keep the three swindlers from attempting a late-night getaway.

Quincannon relocked the door and then picked the latch on the one adjacent. The money was not among Saxe's and Cora Lee's possessions, either. The search of their rooms had been a small hope at best; chances were the greenbacks rested in a money belt around the Cloud Cracker's waist.

But he did find one item of considerable interest, in plain sight on the stand next to the bed: a timetable for Southern Pacific's Central Valley passenger trains, with notations penned in ink at the top. The notations read: *Stockton Limited, Friday, nine a.m. Bainsville.*

This Friday, tomorrow? Probably. Yet, it was unlikely that the trio would be planning to leave by train and in broad daylight. The more probable pattern would be to dismantle the mortar under cover of darkness, load it and the easily transportable items of rainmaking equipment into their wagon, and then vanish in the middle of the night.

Bainsville. Another small farm town some fifteen miles to the north. Ah, so that was their plan. They intended to pack up and escape Delford tonight, driving their wagon to Bainsville, where they would purchase passenger and baggage tickets for themselves if not their equipment. By the time the Delford residents realized what had happened and spread the word, the miscreants would have reached and then departed Stockton for parts unknown.

Quincannon relocked Saxe's door, left the hotel. He hummed a temperance tune under his breath, cheerfully, as he walked to the jail to inform the marshal of his suspicions. He had high hopes that Saxe and his cohorts would in fact attempt to pull out tonight; it would allow him, along with Boxhardt and a deputy or two, to make the arrest. In which case he wouldn't need to wait for the coming of Sheriff Beadle and his deputies, he could return to San Francisco on the morrow.

13

SABINA

The morning mail brought a note from Amity Wellman, reminding Sabina of a Voting Rights for Women supper on Friday evening and urging her to attend if at all possible. A trio of Southern California delegates to the State Woman Suffrage Convention in November had come to the city and would be guest speakers at the supper. It promised to be, Amity wrote, a spirited gathering in preparation for the campaign for a state constitutional amendment to make California the fourth state in the union to give the vote to women.

Sabina, herself an ardent suffragist, had met Amity at a rally the previous autumn. That and their mutual passion for bicycling had made them friends—a friendship that had been put to the test earlier this year when Amity began receiving threatening letters and an attempt was made on her life. Sabina's investigation had unmasked the perpetrator, but in the process opened up a Pandora's box that had had near-tragic results and put a strain on their relations. They had had little enough contact since. Amity's note, warmly signed, indicated that she not only sought Sabina's continued support for the cause, but wished to reestablish the personal bond between them.

Sabina penned a reply stating that she would indeed attend the meeting, looked forward to it and to seeing Amity again, and signed it "Affectionately, Sabina." She addressed an envelope, folded her note inside, and was affixing a stamp when something else brightened her morning—the arrival of a prospective new client.

The card he handed her gave his name as Joshua Brandywine, his profession as "purveyor of fine apparel for the gentleman." It was a name Sabina recognized, for it had appeared in the newspapers often enough, in both social and feature sections as well as in advertisements. Had John been present, he would have been gleefully eager to please Mr. Brandywine. For the man, who in addition to his professional stature was a prominent collector of rare old Chinese objets d'art, was one of San Francisco's wealthiest citizens.

Well-dressed, middle-aged, and corpulent, Brandywine wore a bushy biblical beard but had no hair to speak of above his ears; an expensive cigar jutted from one corner of his wide mouth. He was in a dither, as evidenced by his too red face and a scowl as fierce as John's. It was also evident that he was one of those men who found dealing with a woman on an equal professional basis to be discomfiting, if not downright suspect. He demanded to speak with "the head of the agency," John Quincannon, and was visibly dismayed when she politely told him that Mr. Quincannon was out of town on another investigation, that the agency was in fact two-headed, she being a full partner, and that whatever had brought him here, she was quite capable of attending to it.

To his credit, Brandywine had the good sense not to further express his feelings of male superiority or to take his business elsewhere. He was too upset and too much in need of assistance, and clearly Carpenter and Quincannon, Professional Detective Services, had come highly recommended to him.

"Now, then," Sabina said. "What is the nature of your problem, Mr. Brandywine?"

"Theft. Impossible theft, by God."

"Impossible?"

"Just that. Just that."

"What exactly has been stolen?"

"Chinese antiquities, ten of the most valued and valuable pieces from my collection."

"Please have a seat and tell me what happened."

Mr. Brandywine refused to have a seat. He stalked about the office as John sometimes did when he was flustered, his color darkening to the approximate hue of port wine. Except for the crazy-quilt patterns of smoke from the cigar clenched in his flailing hand, Sabina thought that it might have been possible to see steam rising from the top of his bald dome.

"I tell you, it's impossible!" he cried, his voice rising to two decibels below a shout. "Couldn't have been done. Yet it was, at least twice—there is no other explanation. Maddening! Infuriating!"

"Calm yourself, Mr. Brandywine. I understand how upset

you must be, but there is nothing to be gained in raising your blood pressure."

"I'll thank you not to give me medical advice, young woman!"

Sabina's tenure as a Pink Rose, and her years in partnership with John, had taught her patience and forbearance in dealing with doubting Thomases, outright misogynists, bigots, and fools. She continued to sit quietly with her hands folded on the desktop. Behind her, pale summer sunshine illuminated the window that bore the agency's name in flowing script. The window, open a few inches, admitted various noises from Market Street below: the rumble of a passing cable car, the clatter of dray wagons, the calls of vendors hawking fresh seafood in Sullivan's Fish Stand across the thoroughfare. It also permitted the smoke from Joshua Brandywine's cigar to escape, though not as quickly as she would have liked.

"Very well, sir," she said. "But I can't be of assistance until I know all the facts of the matter."

Mr. Brandywine stopped pacing, but continued the agitated waving of his cigar. "As I told you, I've been robbed. Robbed! Ten pieces taken, half of them irreplaceable, by a thief who seems to have appeared and disappeared in my locked antiquities room like a confounded ghost. No conceivable way to have gotten in through door or windows. None. Impossible."

"Nothing is impossible, sir. The antiquities room is at your home, I assume."

"Yes, yes, where else would it be?"

Sabina said patiently, "When a locked room has been

breached, someone has found a way to breach it. It's as simple as that."

"Simple! It's not simple, it's maddening, it has me at my wit's end—"

"Kindly take your seat and we'll proceed."

Brandywine sputtered a bit more, finally heaved a great tremulous sigh, and planted his substantial posterior in the largest of the client chairs. It creaked audibly under his weight.

Sabina asked, "Where exactly is the antiquities room located?"

"On the second floor. That is what makes the thefts all the more—"

"It contains your entire collection?"

"The finest collection of Sung, Zhou, Han, and Qing dynasty jade and porcelain pieces in the western states, perhaps in the entire nation." A fierce pride replaced some of the man's agitation; his color, Sabina was relieved to see, was less dangerously purplish now. "Nearly three hundred items, many of them exceedingly rare, gathered over the past thirty-five years in this country and on two trips to the Orient."

"You said ten pieces have been stolen?"

"Ten, yes. All small enough to be easily carried off. I became aware of the first theft eight days ago, when I had an opportunity to buy a white Han *bi* in a better state of preservation than one I've owned for many years."

"A *bi*? What is that?"

"A jade artifact, flat, circular, with a hole in the center." Brandywine puffed furiously on his cigar. "I don't spend an inordinate mount of time mooning over individual pieces like some collectors; I derive satisfaction enough in viewing my collection as a whole, with an occasional reexamination of this or that object. I hadn't looked at my *bi* in some time before I discovered it was missing. I couldn't believe it, I thought I must have misplaced it somehow."

"And this led you to make a complete inventory?"

"Naturally. Five other pieces were gone—a Sung rhyton cup, a Han phoenix plaque, a Qianlong famille-rose snuff bottle—"

This was all gibberish to Sabina, though she nodded attentively as if she understood. She asked, "What is the total value of the missing items?"

"Value? Thousands of dollars, but their value to me is far greater than their monetary worth."

"I'm sure it is. Did you report the theft to the police?"

"Of course. Immediately. They did nothing but blunder about. One of the clumsy fools nearly damaged a Shang plate."

John would have said that such was typical police ineptitude. Sabina tended to agree, but she refrained from saying so. She asked, "When did you discover the other four pieces had been stolen?"

"Just last night. Four even more valuable than the first six." Brandywine's anger sparked hot again; he jabbed out the remains of his cigar in the ashtray on John's desk with enough force to spray ashes across the blotter. "Including one of my greatest treasures, an eight-thousand-year-old jade dragon in remarkably fine condition. That is what brought me here, rather than to the Hall of Justice again."

Sabina couldn't resist saying, "A wise decision, sir."

"That," Brandywine said darkly, "remains to be seen."

"Tell me about the antiquities room."

"The only door has a pair of locks of the best manufacture. There is one set of latched French-style windows that can't be reached from the outside, or opened if they could. Can't be opened at all anymore, for that matter—you'll see why when you come to the house."

"How many keys are there to the double locks?"

"Only one for each."

"Do you keep them with you at all times, even at night?"

"No. In the safe in my study. The only time I remove them is when I am about to enter the antiquities room, and I replace them immediately upon locking up again."

"You're certain no one could have gained access to the keys long enough to have them duplicated? Or to make wax impressions?"

"Absolutely certain. No one has the combination to the safe, not even my wife."

"How many people live with you?"

He bristled at the question. "Are you inferring someone in my household is responsible for the thefts?"

"That would seem to be the most likely explanation in a case such as this."

"Well, you're wrong, young woman. Everyone who occupies my home and property is above reproach."

"I would still like you to identify them, please."

"Very well. My wife, Alice. My nephew and ward, Philip— my late brother's son. The housekeeper and cook, Mrs. Endicott. And Grimes, the coachman, gardener, and handyman."

"Are the two servants live-in residents?"

"Yes. Mrs. Endicott has a room off the kitchen, Grimes another in the carriage house. But neither of them has ever exhibited any interest in my collection, or has knowledge of the various pieces. The same is true of my wife and nephew. And my daughter Ruth and her husband."

"Where do they live, may I ask?"

"In Berkeley. Ellis teaches at the university."

"Do they visit often at your home?"

Brandywine's scowl deepened. "What are you implying?"

"Nothing, sir. I am merely asking questions."

"Hmmpf. No, they don't visit often. Too busy. None of my family or my employees has need of money, if that's to be your next question—I am quite generous, if I do say so myself. The thief *must* be an outsider, a professional burglar."

One with specialized knowledge of Chinese curios, Sabina thought, not to mention a foolish and generous nature to have prowled twice and made off with only ten of several hundred valuable items? Highly improbable. But she said only, "How easy would it be for an outsider to gain access to your home?"

"To the grounds, not difficult," Brandywine said. "To the house is another matter. All the doors and windows are kept securely locked at night."

"Have there been any recent signs of illegal entry?"

"No. None. But there are ways to enter homes without leaving traces, I'm sure."

Oh, yes. More than you'd care to know about. "When was the last time anyone other than yourself was inside the antiquities room?"

"More than a week ago. Evander Hightower, an old friend and fellow collector. But I've known Evander for twenty-five years—he is as honest as the day is long. Besides, he was never out of my sight on that or any other occasion when he visited."

"Were you in the room prior to last night's theft?"

"Yes, briefly. Alone. We had no guests. And as always I was careful to make certain both lock bolts were turned when I left again."

The Seth Thomas clock on the wall above John's desk chimed the half hour. Brandywine blinked and peered up at it; then, as if he didn't trust its accuracy, he produced and consulted an embossed gold pocket watch. "Tempus fidgets," he said, frowning.

". . . Excuse me?"

"I've just remembered I have a business meeting in twenty minutes that I cannot afford to miss. It shouldn't last more than an hour. Are you to begin your investigation early this afternoon?"

There being nothing else on her agenda for today, Sabina was quick to say, "Certainly."

"Then I'll expect you at my home promptly at one o'clock." Brandywine pocketed the gold watch and then stood, adjusting the drape of his expensive cutaway coat. "I am not a patient man, Mrs. Carpenter," he said then. "No, not a patient man at all in such an outrageous matter as this. I demand results."

"If at all possible, you shall have them."

"Guaranteed?"

"No reputable detective agency can guarantee anything in

advance except service to the best of their ability. That much I can promise you."

"Very well. What are your fees?"

Sabina told him. John no doubt would have inflated the sum a bit, given Mr. Brandywine's wealth and stature, but she didn't believe in doing business in such a cavalier fashion. To her way of thinking, a client was a client to be treated equally whether a prince or a pauper.

Brandywine said that the fee was acceptable, and surprised her by offering bonuses of five hundred dollars if she successfully resolved the case in forty-eight hours or less, one thousand dollars if within twenty-four. Honesty, she thought, was indeed the best and potentially most rewarding policy.

14

SABINA

Joshua Brandywine's home was an ornate two-story pile high atop Nob Hill, not far from the Blanchford mansion she'd had occasion to visit twice during the course of the Body Snatchers Affair. Mr. Brandywine's was not quite as palatial, nor was the view it commanded of the bay and the piers and anchored ships along the broad sweep of the waterfront below quite as panoramic. It was set well back from the street behind an impressive fence of filigreed black iron pickets, surrounded by flower beds and greensward. The carriage gates in front stood open, evidently in preparation for Sabina's arrival.

The fence, she noted as her hansom entered the grounds, was six feet in height all the way around and the tips of the iron pickets were as sharp as spear points. The tops of the two gate halves were similarly spiked. Climbable, certainly, but at some risk to life and limb.

Through the hack's side window, then, she spied a slender

young man dressed in white trousers and what appeared to be the sleeveless top of a bathing costume engaged in a series of oddly antic maneuvers on the long green to her right. The fellow lay tilted on his back, hands on hips, legs pumping the air as if he were riding an invisible bicycle; then he hopped up in one agile movement and began jumping up and down and flapping his arms like a swan about to take flight.

Calisthenics? If so, he was certainly doing them energetically.

As the hansom rattled past, the young man erupted into a headlong sprint, his strides long and surprisingly swift. Having gone some three hundred feet or so, he slowed, turned, and then raced back at the same lightning speed. After which he dropped to the turf and commenced another round of supine calisthenics.

Joshua Brandywine had evidently been watching for her arrival; he waddled out and stood waiting on the drive, one of his expensive cigars clenched between his teeth, when the driver reined his horse to a halt.

He took her hand and helped her step down, then released it immediately and consulted his gold watch. "One o'clock exactly. Very good. I am a stickler for punctuality, as I told you."

The young man on the green caught Sabina's eye again. He was once more on his feet, bouncing up and down and waving his arms. "Is that your nephew, Mr. Brandywine?"

"Yes, that's Philip. Fancies himself an athlete. Gymnastics, footraces. Sissified nonsense, if you ask me."

She watched the youth do a back flip, then several forward rolls, then a handstand, then leap to his feet and commence another sprint. The exact purpose of the maneuvers may not have been completely comprehensible, but any activity requiring that much dexterity could hardly be termed sissified.

Mr. Brandywine once more peered at his watch. "Come along inside," he said. "Tempus fidgets."

That phrase again, an intentional or unintentional alteration of *tempus fugit*. Evidently it was habitual with him.

He led the way into the house, across a dark foyer to a wide, curving staircase. As they started up, Sabina asked him if his wife was at home.

"Out at one of her club meetings," Brandywine said. "You needn't bother with her, there is nothing she can tell you."

"I may want to speak to her just the same. You have no objection, I trust?"

"I suppose not."

"Your servants? Are they on the premises?"

"Mrs. Endicott is in the kitchen and Grimes somewhere on the grounds. The carriage house, likely—he has a room there. But they have nothing to tell you, either. Nor does my nephew. I've already questioned them, as I told you earlier."

At the top of the stairs Mr. Brandywine turned down a long carpeted hallway to the right and stopped before a heavy oak door with a pair of cast-bronze locks set one above the other. He took two separate keys from his pocket. The locking mechanisms, Sabina noted, were well oiled and the bolts turned with only the faintest of clicks.

"I'll ask you to please not touch any of the artifacts," he said. "Some are quite fragile." Then he opened the door, reached inside to turn a switch that flooded the interior with electric light.

Sabina caught her breath as they entered. It was not unlike walking into an extravagant museum exhibit. The lights gleamed and glittered off the multitude of jade and porcelain artifacts arranged on shelves, tables, pedestals, and inside slant-topped glass cases. So many, large and small, that even though the room was of substantial size, there was space for only a scant few items of furniture—two leather chairs, a small table and a smoking stand set between them, a single low bookcase next to a marble fireplace. Velvet drapes the color of claret wine were drawn across the outer wall opposite.

Mr. Brandywine conducted her through the maze of displays. Despite the gravity of her visit, his passion and his pride of ownership brightened his features and his voice as he pointed out various treasures. There were vases, bowls, cups, wine vessels, small boxes, incense burners, bangles, belt hooks, snuff bottles, the flat circular objects he referred to as *bis*; the carved images of dragons, birds, and coiled serpents; porcelain figures of people and animals painted in intricate detail; other pieces she was unable to identify. All had been lovingly cared for. The porcelain colors and those of the various types of jade—white, dark green, blue, yellow—seemed to glow as with an inner fire.

But she was not here to look at and admire the client's collection. After a single pass-through, she returned to the door to examine the locks and locking plates with a keen eye. Stephen had been an expert with locks, and John was another;

from them and through practical experience, she had learned as much as she would ever need to know.

These locks were obviously custom-made, no doubt by a master locksmith—the kind that could not be opened by means of a skeleton key or a set of lockpicks of the sort John carried. The keyholes and plates bore no marks of tampering, nor was there any trace of wax residue; they were as gleamingly clean as the artifacts. The only way the thief could have entered this way was if he possessed Mr. Brandywine's keys or exact duplicates—which, if the testimony of the purveyor of fine menswear was trustworthy, could not have been managed.

A swishing sound redirected Sabina's attention. Brandywine had opened the dark red drapes to reveal the French-style windows behind them. He beckoned to her, and said when she joined him, "These windows haven't been opened since I bought this house a dozen years ago. Can't be opened, as I told you before."

Sabina examined them closely. The windows were some three feet in height, two leaded panes of glass in each half; a heavy, curved latch that matched the ornate handles fastened the two together.

"And why can't they be opened?" she asked.

"See for yourself. Stand to one side or the other and look through the glass at an angle."

She did that. The glass was less than clean inside and out and slightly opaque as a result, but she had no trouble viewing the thick, rough-textured strips that had been applied to the edges of both halves and to the crack where they joined in the middle.

"Weather stripping," she said.

"More precisely, a permanent seal. Strips of thick rubberized pile bonded to the frames. The windows leaked when it rained and permitted drafts to enter even in dry weather. That is one reason I had them sealed. The other, of course, being security."

The windows were hinged to open outward. Sabina lifted the curved latch, grasped both handles, and pushed hard enough to cause the halves to rattle faintly in their frames. The weather stripping held them fast together.

"You see?" Brandywine said. "Still sealed tight. I checked them myself again this morning."

Sabina replaced the latch around its fastener, then peered out again through the glass. The nephew, Philip, was still performing his athletic rituals on the grass below. Directly beneath the windows was a bed of closely spaced purple flowers at least six feet wide that separated the house wall from the greensward.

"That flower bed below. Soft earth?"

"Yes. That is another reason why the windows are not the means by which the thief entered this room. There is no way to reach them except by ladder—not even a monkey could climb the wall—and if a ladder had been placed in the bed, the delphiniums would have been crushed and there would have been deep indentations as well as footprints. There was no such damage when I examined it this morning. And Grimes would have reported it to me if there had been previously."

The fireplace was not the answer, either. It was no longer in use, had in fact been sealed—evidently another casualty of

Mr. Brandywine's dislike of drafts. The room, and likely the rest of the house, was gas heated.

Nor was there any sort of secret room or passageway between the walls—an improbability, but one that had to be considered. Her client had assured Sabina of this, but she did some random tapping and searching to make certain.

When she was done with that, she perused the spines of the books in the small case. "Are these all you have on the subject of Chinese antiquities?" she asked him.

"Except for one or two downstairs in the library where I sometimes do my reading. Why do you ask?"

"No particular reason. Successful detectives are curious creatures, Mr. Brandywine."

There was nothing more to be examined here. Sabina said she would like to interview Mrs. Endicott. Brandywine, after double-locking the antiquities room, accompanied her downstairs and summoned the housekeeper to the library—a large room lined with books in glass cases and otherwise filled with a refectory table and dark leather furniture arranged before a massive fieldstone fireplace.

The gray-haired servant answered Sabina's questions readily and, it seemed, honestly. As her employer had indicated, she had no information that might shed light on the thefts.

"And now, Mrs. Carpenter?" Brandywine said after dismissing the housekeeper. He looked and sounded impatient. Tempus fidgets.

"A look around outside. Alone, if you don't mind."

"As you wish."

Outside, she went around to the side wall beneath the

antiquities room and stood peering upward. The house wall was sheer all the way up past the French-style windows to a small window beneath the eaves; there were no hand- or footholds of any kind, and the white-painted boards appeared to be free of marks. No, not even a monkey could have climbed it.

A study of the flower beds for a dozen feet in either direction also bore out Brandywine's claim. Neither the purple delphiniums nor the soft earth had been disturbed. The beds were too wide for a ladder, even a long one of the sort painters used, to have been placed at an angle at the edge of the green and then climbed from there. And if further proof were needed, there were no telltale indentations in the grass.

"Hello. Are you the lady detective my uncle hired?"

Sabina turned. The nephew, Philip, had come up softly behind her. At close quarters, the lad—he was not long past the age of legal majority—was the picture of youthful health and fitness. Towheaded, muscles rippling in his bare arms and shoulders, his face damply aglow from his exertions, a grave smile curving his mouth.

"I am. How did you know?"

"He grumbled to me when he came home about having to settle, as he put it, for a woman and hoped he hadn't made a mistake in doing so. What is the world coming to, and all that." The youth chuckled. "My name is Philip. But then you already know that, I'm sure."

"Yes. Mine is Sabina Carpenter."

"Well, I'm charmed, even if Uncle isn't."

"Thank you."

"Have you any idea how someone could have gotten into the antiquities room? If someone did, that is."

"If?"

"Uncle said it couldn't be done. And his memory isn't what it once was, by his own admission. He might have sold or traded the items he claims are missing."

"Does he do much selling and trading?"

"I don't know. He's closemouthed about his hobby."

"He seems convinced ten items were stolen."

Philip shrugged. "Then I suppose they must have been, somehow."

"Do you know anything about Chinese artifacts, Philip?"

"Not a thing. They don't interest me in the slightest."

"What does interest you?"

"Sports." Excitement brightened the lad's hazel eyes. "Track and field, primarily. Sometimes I do my training with friends at the Olympic Club, sometimes here by myself."

"Training?"

"For the Olympic Games in Paris when the century turns. I had hoped to be able to compete in this year's games in Athens—the first international Olympic games in modern times, you know. But Uncle wouldn't allow it. He said I was too young."

"You must have been disappointed."

"Yes, but I suppose he had a point. I'll be in even better condition in four years, and old enough to make my own plans and decisions."

"What events do you hope to participate in?"

"The sixty-meter and one-hundred-meter races. The one-hundred-ten-meter high hurdles. Gymnastics, too, if possible. I'm sure I'll be able to qualify for at least one event, but even if I don't, I'll attend the games as a spectator. It's sure to be a thrilling experience."

"Your uncle doesn't seem to share your enthusiasm for sports."

"Not at all. He didn't even want me to join the Olympic Club, even though important men such as Charles Crocker and Leland Stanford are members. But then we all have different passions, different skills, don't we."

"That we do. Good luck to you, Philip."

"And to you, Mrs. Carpenter."

The youth loped off. Sabina watched after him for a moment, then returned to the front of the house. The wide carriage lane looped around on the opposite side and led to the carriage house at the rear. A light wind had begun to blow in from the bay. As she hurried along, the breeze carried the familiar booming sound of a horn as one of the fast coastal steamers drew away from a pier along the Embarcadero.

In front of the open doors to the carriage house, a man she assumed was Grimes stood industriously polishing the brightwork on a handsome Concord buggy. A small mongrel dog sat companionably nearby. The animal cocked its head, gave Sabina a brief study, apparently decided she was of no interest, and yawned. Grimes was in his thirties, with long hair and chin whiskers of a deep russet color—a brawny specimen who appeared even more fit than young Philip, his chest and shoulders broad, muscled arms as thick as saplings. Coachman, gardener, handyman. And a more than adequate bodyguard, no doubt, if his employer ever had need of one.

Sabina identified herself. Grimes gave her a brief, not quite impudent look and allowed as how Mr. Brandywine had told him he'd hired a detective. "Didn't say it was a woman, though."

She had nothing to say to that.

"Never seen him so upset," Grimes said. "You think you can find out how the thief got into that special room of his?"

She countered by asking, "Do you have any idea how it was done?"

"No, ma'am. Not hardly."

"I understand you have a room here in the carriage house. You've neither heard nor seen any sign of an intruder on the grounds?"

"None. And I would have, I think, if there'd been one. I'm not a heavy sleeper, and Pard here has keen ears. So does Mabel, the coach horse. Set up a racket over a cat more'n once, both of 'em."

"Has Mr. Brandywine ever invited you to view his collection?"

"Not me. He don't allow anyone in that room that I know about." Grimes' smile was just a little bent when he added, "Only times I've ever been inside the house was for a kitchen meal or when repairs were needed."

"Do you have keys to any of the doors?"

"No, ma'am. Never been trusted with 'em."

"And you know nothing about Chinese artifacts?"

"Me? Not a blessed thing."

"Have you ever seen any of Mr. Brandywine's, at any time?"

"Well, yeah, once. In the rig here, when I was driving him home, he showed me one he'd just bought—a carved dragon he said was thousands of years old. Pretty enough, I guess, but nothing I'd fuss over." A belated thought seemed to strike the man. His eyes narrowed, his whiskers twitched. "Say, you don't think I had anything to do with those thefts?"

"Your employer assured me you didn't."

"And that's a fact. I never so much as stole a nickel in my life, nor ever will. I like my job, and what Mr. Brandywine pays me takes care of all my needs."

Too great a protest? Sabina reserved judgment for the time being.

"There are ladders in the carriage house, I trust," she said.

"Ladders? Why?"

"I may have need of the tallest you have."

"What for?"

"For a close look at the antiquities-room windows."

"Waste of time. Those windows can't be opened."

"So I've been told more than once. I'd still like them examined."

"Can't put a ladder up in the beds over there without crushing some of the plants," Grimes said, frowning. "Mrs. Brandywine won't like it."

"Nonetheless, I think it's necessary."

"You're not thinking of climbing up a tall ladder yourself . . . a lady nice dressed like you?"

"Not I." She was athletic enough to have done so, but even dressed in less expensive and confining clothing, climbing tall ladders in public was an activity a well-bred lady simply did not indulge in. One day, perhaps, when the emancipation of women was complete, but at this time it was best to observe some of the rigid standards of social etiquette.

"Well, I won't do it," Grimes said. "Or put a ladder up for anybody else. Not without Mr. Brandywine's permission."

"I had no intention of asking you to do either task . . . yet. You do have a ladder tall enough to reach those windows?"

"Yes, but like I said—"

Sabina gave him the benefit of a small smile, thanked him, and left him still wearing his disapproving frown.

Mrs. Endicott answered her ring at the house and showed her into the library, where Joshua Brandywine was waiting. "Well, young woman?" he demanded in clipped tones. "Do you have any theories yet?"

"I'd rather not say at the moment."

"Why the devil not?"

"Our agency's policy is never to discuss an investigation until completed."

Brandywine emitted a faint snorting sound. "Which means, I expect, that you're still as much in the dark as I am."

"Not necessarily, sir," Sabina said. Before he could respond to that, she said, "I'd like your permission to have the antiquities-room windows examined from the outside, even though it will mean disturbing the flower beds."

"What's that? What for? I have already told you—"

"I believe it's necessary. *Do* I have your permission?"

"Examined when? By whom?"

"Tomorrow morning. By an associate of mine."

"Tomorrow? Why not today?"

"Because it can't be arranged today."

Mr. Brandywine hemmed and hawed and finally gave in. "This notion of yours had better produce results," he said portentously. "If it doesn't, I'll see to it you pay for any and all damage to my property."

"Agreed."

He once again consulted his gold watch. "Is there anything more you want to ask me? Or to look at?"

"Not at present."

"Then I'll ring for Grimes to drive you downtown."

The cushions in the Concord buggy were well padded and comfortable. And conducive to cogitation. Sabina's response to her client's comment that she was as much in the dark as he had not been evasive or dissembling. She had an idea of how the seemingly impossible trick of breaching the antiquities room and making off with the ten artifacts had been worked. Tomorrow she would know if her surmise was correct.

When they neared Market Street she directed Grimes to cross over and turn west on Folsom. Her destination was the blacksmith shop owned by Whit Slattery. Upon arrival there, she asked Grimes if he minded waiting while she went inside, then dropping her back at Market and Second. "Not at all, ma'am," he said. "I got nothing else to do, and Mr. Brandywine's instructions were to drive you wherever you wanted to go."

Blacksmithing was Whit's primary profession, but he also doubled as a part-time operative whenever Carpenter and Quincannon, Professional Detective Services, had need of one. John had met him during the course of a Secret Service investigation several years ago, and recruited him when he learned that Slattery had been a member of the U.S. Army assigned to guard valuables in transit over the Panama Railroad during the revolutionary activity in 1885. He had proved to be trustworthy, quick-witted, and implacable when necessary.

He was glad to be of assistance, as always, even though the task was a simple one that required neither brains nor brawn. Sabina readily accepted his offer to come by for her in the morning and drive them to the Brandywine home.

It was after four when Grimes delivered her to her next destination, the Commercial Street offices of the *Morning Call*. She spent fifteen minutes in the company of Ephraim Ballard, the old man in the dusty green eyeshade who presided over the newspaper's morgue and who supplied her with the back issue she sought. The information she read therein to refresh her memory added strength to her theory.

From the *Morning Call,* she walked to Market Street. The sidewalks, as usual at this time of day, were packed with humanity. Everyone seemed to be in a hurry these days, particularly those men who had left their places of business early in order to achieve a head start on the evening Cocktail Route ritual. As she made her way to the Western Union office, Sabina was mindful of careless jostlers and the pickpockets and purse snatchers who were bold enough to ply their felonious trades in broad daylight on downtown streets.

There were three more collect wires waiting. Two were in answer to John's queries, one from the Pinkerton branch office in Dallas, the other from the detective agency in Little

Rock. The third wire had been sent by Grass Valley Sheriff Hezekiah Thorpe. Only that one contained tersely worded new information of interest. Grave interest, perhaps.

TRIAL DATE MOVED UP TO JULY 17 STOP LADY STILL MUM STOP JG MISSING SINCE LAST NIGHT WHEREABOUTS UNKNOWN STOP

H THORPE

Whereabouts unknown? Jeffrey Gaunt might have gone anywhere, it was true, but his most likely destination once he learned Lady One-Eye's trial date had been set for ten days hence was obvious. As was his purpose, if in fact he had come to San Francisco.

The prospect didn't frighten Sabina. But it did make her even more wary and vigilant on her way to the office and then home afterward.

15

QUINCANNON

He took his supper at a side-street establishment called the Elite Café, which advertised "the best home-cooked meals in Delford" (if this was true, the worst were probably lethal), and then at a quarter of seven he walked down to the rail yards.

Some of the day's heat had eased, but the sky was still hazed and cloudless. Not a breath of wind stirred the parched air. A crowd had begun to assemble under the locust trees near the watchman's shack—men, women, a few children. The mood was anything but festive; facial expressions on the adults ranged from wary optimism to half-sullen pessimism. The trio of swindlers had correctly gauged the tenor of the town, a primary factor in their decision to flee tonight; when they failed again to bring rain, as they surely would, the more militant among the disillusioned might well take to cooking tar and gathering feathers.

As Quincannon approached the shack he could hear a

rumbling, fluttering noise coming from within, not unlike the activity of several hives of hornets. It had an impressive sound, as befitted a "miracle cloud-cracking machine," but of course it was nothing more than the workings of the steam boiler and galvanic battery. Virulent yellow gas still issued from the stovepipe jutting above the roof: a combination of hydrogen and oxygen produced, no doubt, by mingling muriatic acid, zinc, and a little hydrogen, which was then pumped skyward through the boiler. The mortar rockets would contain a similar and equally worthless chemical mixture.

Quincannon was about to take up a position near the mortar platform when the shack's door opened and two men emerged. One was Mortimer Rollins; the other, heavyset, bearded, with a flowing silver-black mane, would be the notorious Leopold Saxe. Both were in shirtsleeves, sweating profusely from the heat inside, and each carried a pair of long, slender mortar shells. Cora Lee Johnson, dressed now in a fancy green-and-blue lace-trimmed outfit, a squash-blossom necklace at her throat, followed after them, smiling and waving at the crowd. Even though she, too, had been inside the shack, she looked cool and dry and unruffled.

Saxe and Rollins brought their burdens to the platform, laid them at the foot of the slingshot cannon. Quincannon joined them at that point. He said, "Good evening, gentlemen, Mrs. Daks," and doffed his derby to the woman. "Preparations for tonight's entertainment are nearly complete, I see."

Saxe bristled visibly at this. He was an imposing figure up close, as most successful confidence men were; his eyes, of such a dark brown hue they seemed almost black, were piercing and his manner imperious. "Entertainment? Hardly that, sir. Hardly that. Drought-breaking is a serious business."

"I have no doubt of it."

"And who might you be, may I ask?"

"This is Mr. Quincannon, Leonide," Cora Lee said, "the San Francisco newspaperman I told you about."

"Ah, yes." Saxe's irritation vanished behind a mask of good fellowship. He pumped Quincannon's hand vigorously. "A pleasure, my good sir. I am in your debt for saving my wife and assistant from harm this afternoon."

"Not at all. Mr. Goodland was too far under influence to have inflicted much harm on anyone."

Saxe accepted the glib half truth with a nod. "A ticklish situation, nonetheless," he said. Then he frowned and called out to Rollins, "Here, Ben, what're you doing?"

The smaller man had climbed onto the platform, was picking up one of the rocket shells. Before he answered he began inserting the missile into the cannon's muzzle. "Loading the mortar, as you can plainly see."

"There is time enough for that."

"I'd rather have done with it now."

Saxe said to Quincannon, sounding irritated again, "Insolent fellow. I may have to hire a new assistant. Now if you'll excuse me, sir, there is more work to be done inside. We'll talk again later, eh?"

"Oh, yes. We'll have much to say to each other, I'm sure."

The confidence trickster turned away. Rollins, who had finished loading the mortar, leaned over to take Cora Lee's hand

and help her onto the platform. Then he dropped down beside Quincannon, favored him with a curt head bow, and followed Saxe into the shack. The door shut firmly behind him.

Quincannon retraced his steps past the platform, where Cora Lee was now soaking the tip of a long firebrand in kerosene. Under a locust tree, while he fed tobacco into his briar, he saw Aram Kasabian, Mayor Parnell, and Tom Boxhardt approaching. O. H. Goodland was not with them, nor was he anywhere else in the vicinity.

The three men drew Quincannon aside, out of earshot of the other townsfolk. "We saw you talking to those two," the banker said, fanning his red face with a pudgy hand, "and wondered why."

"A testing of the waters, you might say."

"I'm not sure I—"

"There isn't a speck of worry in Saxe, though I detected some in Rollins. They know that they have played out their string here and they're planning to skip town tonight."

"Are you sure?"

"Sure enough." Quincannon explained to Kasabian and Purcell about the railroad timetable he'd found in Saxe's room, and his inference that the trio intended to slip out of the hotel after midnight, quickly hitch and load the dougherty wagon, and head for Bainsville.

"We'll be ready for 'em," Boxhardt vowed. "How many extra men you figure I ought to deputize, Mr. Quincannon?"

"Your regular deputy ought to be enough."

"You'll be there, too?"

"I wouldn't miss it."

"We can wait and watch here in the trees."

"Yes, and I suggest the three of us make our way here one at a time, carefully, between nine and ten to set up our vigil."

"That's what we'll do, then."

"The only possible fly in the ointment is Mr. Goodland. Where is he now, do any of you know?"

"He was in his room a few minutes ago," Parnell said. "I stopped by to have a word with him."

"Sober?"

"More or less, but surly and pacing like a cat. I warned him to stay away from the Cloud Cracker, but it won't surprise me if he takes it in his head to come out here tonight—"

Boxhardt said thinly, "Already has. Look."

Quincannon and the other two men turned. O. H. Goodland was striding purposefully toward the shack from the opposite direction. Even at a distance he appeared grim visaged and hard eyed. His hands were empty, but he wore his cowhide coat buttoned at the waist; it was impossible to tell if he was armed or not.

Quincannon growled "Thunderation!" under his breath and then called out Goodland's name. The wheat farmer took no notice. He was at the shack's door now, and he beat on it once with a closed fist. It opened immediately. And immediately he pushed his way inside, slamming the door shut behind him.

"Oh Lord," Kasabian moaned, "if he's come here to do something foolish—"

"Good citizens of Delford! Cover your ears and cast your

eyes to the heavens! Your parched land will soon be drenched in a life-giving downpour, the time is close at hand now!"

These words came from Cora Lee Johnson atop the platform. They quieted the crowd and brought all eyes her way, momentarily froze Quincannon and the other three men in place. She had put a match to the firebrand, he saw, and now stood with it poised and flaming over the mortar's fuse vent.

Boxhardt said in an awed voice, "By grab, the woman's fixin' to fire that thing all by herself—"

He broke off as Cora Lee lit the fuse, then dropped the firebrand, raised her skirts, and scurried down off the platform in unladylike haste.

In the next instant there was a tremendous concussive *whump!* The slingshot cannon bucked, the platform shuddered, and the chemical rocket Rollins had inserted earlier hurtled skyward with an earsplitting whistle. After several hundred feet the missile arced, then burst with a flash that unleashed streams of colored smoke.

Quincannon saw this at the edge of his vision; he was moving by then, his attention on the shack's closed door. It remained closed until he had gained the far end of the platform and then it popped open to reveal Mortimer Rollins. The mustached trickster stepped out, yanked the door shut behind him; when he spied Quincannon's little group he began gesticulating wildly. His handsome face was a sweat-sheened mask of distress.

"Marshal Boxhardt! Mayor!" he shouted. "Come quickly!" On the last word he spun on his heel, lunged back to the door.

By the time Quincannon and the others rushed up behind him, he had the knob in both hands and was rattling it frantically. "Locked—Goodland's locked it!"

"What the devil happened?" Boxhardt demanded.

"He made threats, drew his pistol and ordered me to leave . . ." Rollins punished the door again. "Leonide! Are you all right?"

From inside a muffled voice cried in terror, "No, Goodland, no, don't shoot! Don't kill me!"

Quincannon and the marshal roughly pushed past Rollins, in close to the door. Several other men, including Kasabian and Parnell, formed a crowded half circle behind them.

Another cry came from within. "Please, spare my life!"

Seconds later there was the report of a pistol.

Quincannon's reaction was immediate. He hurled his weight against the door, with sufficient force to send it crashing inward. He was off balance as he burst inside; staggered and righted himself just in time to avoid tripping over O. H. Goodland, who was huddled on one knee on the uneven plank floor. Between the wheat farmer and the rainmaking apparatus at the far wall, Leopold Saxe lay supine in a twisted, motionless sprawl. The front of his ruffled shirt was splotched with blood.

Goodland appeared to be hurt; pain contorted his face and his left hand cradled the back of his head. Held limply in his right hand was a Colt New Pocket revolver. Quincannon yanked the weapon free of the farmer's unresisting grasp.

On one knee beside Saxe, Rollins said heavily, "He's dead. Shot through the heart."

The door under the boiler stood open to reveal the pulsing flames within. With the shack's single window closed and sealed, the heat in the room was stifling. Quincannon breathed shallowly through his mouth as he scanned the dim confines. The only light came from the fire and from a single coal-oil lamp, but his sharp eyes picked out the glint of something on the floor near one of the earthenware crocks. He sidestepped Goodland and the dead man, bent to scoop up the small object—and almost dropped it because it was hot to the touch.

A wailing voice rose from outside: "Let me through, oh please let me through!"

The knot of men clogging the doorway parted to permit Cora Lee Johnson to enter. When she saw Saxe she flung herself down beside him, just as Lily Dumont had beside the corpse of Jack O'Diamonds in Grass Valley; caught up one of his hands and hugged it to her bosom, sobbing.

Quincannon glanced at the object he'd found. It was a spent cartridge shell. He drew out his handkerchief, wrapped the casing in it, held it loosely until it was cool enough to slip into his coat pocket.

O. H. Goodland still clutched his scalp, grimacing, blinking now as if his eyes refused to focus properly. Dizziness overcame him when he tried to stand; he sank down again to one knee. "My head . . . feels as though it'd been cracked like an eggshell . . ."

Rollins said, "He must have slipped and fallen somehow when he shot poor Leonide."

"Shot? I didn't shoot anyone . . ."

Boxhardt stepped forward, relieved Quincannon of the

Colt's revolver. He sniffed the barrel, then turned it over in his hand. "This here's your weapon, Mr. Goodland. Recently fired."

"Tell you, I didn't shoot anyone."

"He's guilty as sin," Rollins said. "There was no one else here, no one else could have done it. You see that, don't you, Marshal?"

"I see it," Boxhardt agreed grimly. "Mr. Goodland, I got no choice but to arrest you for the crime of murder."

Quincannon did not accompany the marshal and his prisoner to the jailhouse. Nor did he follow Rollins and a still-sobbing Cora Lee Johnson to the hotel. Instead he remained at the shack until the town's undertaker arrived to claim Leopold Saxe's remains and Kasabian, Mayor Parnell, and the rest of the shocked Delfordians had dispersed. Then he shut himself inside.

The first thing he did was to examine the door and its sliding bolt. Then he searched among the jars of chemicals, spare rockets, and other items that littered the floor in the vicinity of the boiler and crocks; searched every nook and cranny until he satisfied himself that there was nothing else to be found, least of all the coalition's two thousand dollars. The money hadn't been on Saxe's person, either; he had given the body a quick frisk while Boxhardt was occupied in arresting the dazed wheat farmer.

From the rail yards he went to the Western Union office,

where he sent a night wire to his contact at the Pinkerton Agency in Chicago. The wire asked specific questions and ended with the words URGENT REPLY NEEDED. If the Pinks operative heeded this, as he surely would, an answering wire would arrive by tomorrow noon.

Meanwhile, tonight's vigil would be held as planned. Rollins and Cora Lee may or may not still intend to slip away during the night. If they did, they would join O. H. Goodland under lock and key in a jail cell. Otherwise, their arrest would come on the morrow.

Warm, dusty darkness was settling when Quincannon left the telegraph office. Word of the shooting had spread quickly; gaslit Main Street was packed with citizens discussing the Cloud Cracker's violent demise. They would have a great deal more to discuss within the next twenty-four hours, he thought as he made his way to the marshal's office. And they weren't the only ones for whom there were surprises in store.

Within twenty-four hours the name most often spoken in Delford would not be Leonide Daks/Leopold Saxe or O. H. Goodland. It would be John Frederick Quincannon.

Rollins and Cora Lee made their escape attempt at two-thirty A.M.

Stationed in the locust trees with Boxhardt and his deputy, Quincannon spied the pair first. They were moving shadows at the far side of the field where the dougherty wagon and roan horse were picketed, having evidently left the hotel by the rear entrance and circled around through the back streets.

His hunch was that they intended to abandon all the bogus rainmaking apparatus, including the mortar, and slip away quickly and quietly into the night, and it proved to be correct. Rollins went directly to the wagon, while Cora Lee fetched the placid dray horse. They worked in tandem to harness the animal, performing the task with the dispatch of long practice. The pair were just climbing up onto the seat when Quincannon and the other two men opened the dark lanterns they carried and hurried out of hiding.

The confidence tricksters feigned shock and indignation at first, as well as surprise when Quincannon revealed himself to be a detective hired by Aram Kasabian. Rollins claimed that "Mrs. Daks" was so distraught over her husband's death that she couldn't bear to remain in Delford any longer. "I am escorting her to Stockton, where she has a relative," he lied. "Leonide's murderer is locked in a cell. There is no good reason why either of us should remain here or for you to detain us—"

"You're forgetting the Delford Coalition's two thousand dollars," Quincannon said.

"If you think we're making off with that, you're mistaken. We have no idea where the money is."

"My husband insisted on keeping all our funds," Cora Lee said, "and he was very secretive about where."

"Hid it someplace inside the wagon, mayhap?"

"With it sitting out here in an open field? No, he never would have taken such a risk."

"So a thorough search of the wagon would be fruitless."

"Completely fruitless, I'm sure."

"And I'm sure that it won't be. We'll find the two thousand dollars, Cora Lee, wherever you and Mortimer here hid it."

She gasped and Rollins stiffened at the use of their true names. They knew then that the game was up and any more protest would be futile. When Marshal Boxhardt informed them that Sheriff Beadle was bringing fugitive warrants for their arrest on multiple charges of fraud and placed them in restraints, they lapsed into sullen silence.

The hiding place of the coalition money, whether devised by one of them or by Leopold Saxe, was clever, but not clever enough to fool Quincannon's canny brain. The cash was not concealed anywhere in the wagon proper. He found it in a pouch attached to the underside of one of the harness traces.

16

SABINA

Whit Slattery came for her promptly at eight-thirty Friday morning, not in his blacksmith's wagon but in a small, calèche-topped carriage that he must have rented or borrowed. He also wore a coat and cravat, despite the task he would be performing. When she commented on this, he said laconically, "Can't go bringing a lady to Nob Hill dressed in my work garb." Sabina smiled at that. Gallantry was another of Whit's virtues.

The front gates to the Brandywine property were once again open. Philip was not out doing his calisthenics today; the greensward was empty. Nor did the purveyor of fine apparel for the gentleman come out to meet them when they drew to a stop on the turnaround near the front entrance, as he had the day before. He was waiting in the library.

With him was a gray-haired woman whom he introduced as his wife, Alice. She must have been quite a belle in her youth,

Sabina thought, and time had been much kinder to her than it had to her husband; she was still slender, still attractive in her late forties or early fifties. But she carried herself with the kind of matronly, vaguely absent air Sabina had seen before, that of a woman to whom motherhood had been the focal point of her life and who had been vaguely lost since her child left the nest. She no doubt doted on Philip, but he wouldn't mean the same to her as if he were her own son, and he, too, would soon be gone. Her days then would be entirely taken up with time fillers such as garden parties and women's club activities.

Once Whit had been introduced—the client acknowledged him with a curt nod and thereafter ignored him—Mrs. Brandywine said to Sabina, "Joshua has told me of your intention to trample my delphinium beds. Must you do that?"

"I'm afraid so. We'll be careful to create as little damage as possible."

"And you'll replace any plants that are damaged?"

"At our expense, if the task proves to be fruitless."

"If it does," her husband said ominously, "and you fail to solve the dilemma quickly, I will terminate our arrangement without payment of the balance of your fee."

"So you informed me yesterday, sir."

"Get on with it, then. Grimes is waiting for you at the carriage house. I have canceled an appointment and a luncheon in order to be on hand this morning, and I expect . . . no, I demand results."

Outside, Sabina led the way around toward the carriage house. "Not a very pleasant gent, is he," Whit said.

"Pompous is the word."

"Well, I hope this business turns out the way you hope it will. He meant what he said inside."

"Yes. He did."

A tall extension ladder leaned against the wall of the carriage house; Grimes lounged near it, smoking a cigarette that he quickly discarded when he saw them approaching. He eyed Whit, nodded when Sabina gave his name; neither man offered to shake hands. The ladder was some eight feet in length, the extension another four or five, and it looked to be heavy, but Grimes shook his head when Whit offered to help him carry it. As if to demonstrate his strength and agility, he hoisted it under one arm and brought it effortlessly to the side of the house where the antiquities room was located, his dog trotting along at his heels.

"I'll set it up," Grimes said. "Do the least amount of damage that way."

He proceeded to lay the ladder in the grass at the edge of the flower beds, after which he spent two or three minutes creating as much space as possible among the close-set delphinium plants. Then, carefully, he picked the ladder up again, extended it, carried it on tiptoe through the flower bed, and leaned it gently at an angle against the house wall. Despite his precautions, he was unable to avoid crushing two or three of the plants. The top of the ladder reached to just below the bottom windowsills.

Back on the grass, he urged Whit to be careful and then stood back with his arms folded. He and Sabina watched as Whit stepped gingerly to the ladder, managing not to murder more than one additional delphinium on the way, and made short work of the climb up. Balanced at the top he began carrying out Sabina's instructions, probing the frames, the thick rough-textured pile sealing them, the leaded-glass panes.

"What's he looking for anyway?" Grimes asked.

Sabina sidestepped the question by asking one of her own. "Are you the one who weather stripped the windows?"

"No. That was done before my time. Professional job."

"That small window above the others. What is behind it?"

"Attic."

"For storage or some other purpose?"

"Storage. Old furniture and the like. Most of it I hauled up there myself—part of my job."

After some minutes Whit finished his examination and climbed back down. When he was on the grass, Grimes said, "Didn't find anything, did you?"

Whit said nothing.

The handyman took his silence to mean he hadn't. "Knew you wouldn't," he said, and stepped into the flower bed once again to remove the ladder.

But Whit *had* found something, just the sort of tampering Sabina had expected he might. In a lowered voice he told her about it in detail on their way back to the front entrance. Now she knew beyond any doubt how the antiquities room had been breached. The question now was how the thief had gotten to the windows without use of a ladder, and she was fairly sure she knew the answer to that, too.

Joshua Brandywine was alone in the library, puffing on a cigar and paging through one of his tomes on Chinese curios, when Mrs. Endicott showed them in. He put the book down and popped to his feet. "All finished with that ladder business, I take it. Did you or didn't you find anything?"

"We did."

"Well? What?"

"Patience, Mr. Brandywine."

"Patience, my eye. I told you before, I am not a patient man." As if to validate the fact, he stamped his foot in a manner that reminded Sabina of a temperamental horse.

"Rather than explain," Sabina said, "Mr. Slattery and I will demonstrate in the antiquities room. But we've somewhere else to go first."

"What's that? Where?"

"The attic."

"The— What for?"

"You'll soon see."

Muttering to himself, Brandywine led them up the curving staircase to the second floor and then a straight staircase behind a closed door and into the attic. The low-ceilinged space had not been wired for electricity; he lit a pair of gas wall lamps that provided just enough feeble light to see and navigate by.

The attic was dusty, decorated with cobwebs and cluttered with the usual jumble of castoffs. Sabina made her way through the maze to the far wall, moving aside a heavy iron bedstead in order to reach the small grit-streaked window directly above the antiquities room. The window was held shut by a simple catch. When she flipped it and nudged the glass, the window opened outward soundlessly on oiled hinges.

She looked closely at the bedstead. Dust coated it, except

for a section on one of the thick frame supports that had been rubbed more or less clean. Now she had the rest of the solution.

Turning to Mr. Brandywine, she asked, "I take it your nephew is not home at present?"

"Philip? No, he left for some sort of sports activity just after breakfast. Why are you asking about him?"

"Yesterday you told me you don't approve of his interest in sports. And he told me later that he aspires to participate in the Olympic Games in Paris in nineteen hundred, and that he plans to attend even if he is unable to compete."

"The boy is much too young to go gallivanting halfway round the world on a foolish whim."

"So you've told him you refuse to finance such a journey?"

"Yes, I— What are you getting at, young woman?"

"That it was Philip who stole your artifacts. In order to finance such a trip himself."

"That . . . that is preposterous!"

"I'm sorry, sir, but it's the only possible explanation."

"How the devil could he have gotten into the antiquities room?"

"By utilizing one of his gymnastic skills."

"Skill? What skill?"

"A newspaper article about the Olympic Games I reread yesterday identified the gymnastic events in detail. They include synchronized team floor calisthenics, running, and high jumping. And one other."

"Well?"

"Rope climbing," Sabina said.

Mr. Brandywine wagged his head in dismay.

"It was a simple matter," Sabina went on, "for Philip to slip up here in the middle of the night, open this window, secure one end of a strong rope to this iron bedframe, then climb out and shinny down the side wall to the antiquities-room windows below. I suspect a more careful search of the attic will uncover the rope."

Brandywine still didn't quite believe it. "How in heaven's name could the boy get through latched and sealed windows while dangling at the end of a rope?"

"Easily enough, for a lad as fit and agile as Philip. We'll go downstairs now for the demonstration."

On the second floor, Sabina and Whit waited while Brandywine fetched his keys from the study safe, then the three of them proceeded to the antiquities room. With a hand that was not quite steady, the menswear tycoon opened the double locks and led them inside.

Sabina took the lead here, crossing among the glittering displays to open the velvet drapes. "To begin with," she said then, "Philip would have committed his burglaries well after midnight, when he was certain everyone was fast asleep. What he did after climbing down from the attic was this: he braced both feet—likely bare to avoid leaving marks—against the wall to hold himself in place next to the windows. Hanging onto the rope with one hand, he then unsealed and unlatched the windows—"

"You make an apparent impossibility seem like child's play. *How* did he open the sealed windows?"

She lifted the curved latch bar that held the two window

halves together, and then nodded to Whit. He grasped the handle on the right half and pushed outward with considerably more force than Sabina had used the previous afternoon. Even so, he had to shove hard a second time before there came a faint ripping sound and the windows half swung open.

Mr. Brandywine gawked at the opening, amazement written plain on his florid countenance. "But . . . but I don't understand. The weather stripping—"

"Was sliced through along the three sides of this half, and up the middle where it joined the other half," Whit said, speaking for the first time. "With a knife that had a long, thin, flexible blade. He maneuvered the blade into the crack between the two halves, then upward to free the latch inside here. Easy enough, then, for him to swing through."

"And with the aid of matches or a small candle," Sabina added, "he was able to pick and choose artifacts small enough to carry in his pockets. Doubtless making his selections based on the reading of one or more of your books on Chinese curios left in the library."

The menswear mogul was still incredulous. "But I tested those windows myself. So did you, Mrs. Carpenter. They held fast both times."

"The reason for that is also easily explained, as Mr. Slattery discovered in his examination of the weather stripping. Each time Philip was done with his pilfering, he positioned the latch bar so it could be manipulated back into place with the knife blade. After which he swung out on the rope, braced himself, and drew the window shut. Once that was accomplished, and before climbing back up to the attic, he inserted clear, fast-drying glue—squirted from a tube, probably—into the slits in the weather stripping, thus creating an effective temporary bond. He counted on the fact that there would be no attempt to use excessive force to open the window half from within because of the potential damage to the weather stripping. To carry out his second theft, he simply reslit the glued sections in order to enter, then reglued them after exiting. With the two window halves tightly joined, the thin slits and the clear dried glue were invisible when viewed through the glass from inside and at a distance from outside. The refastened latch completed the illusion that the windows had not been tampered with. Only upon close inspection was the tampering evident."

Mr. Brandywine believed it now. Only a dolt confronted with irrefutable proof could have denied the truth, and whatever else her client might be, he was not a dolt. His color had darkened again to the dangerously purple hue; his mouth was set in angry lines. "That young whelp," he said. "If he has already sold those antiquities—"

"My guess is he hasn't, that they are also hidden somewhere in the attic. But in the event he has sold them, what do you intend to do?"

"That is none of your concern."

"Perhaps not. But I wouldn't be too hard on him, sir. Lads with passionate dreams often make foolish mistakes."

"Don't tell me how to discipline a member of my family," he snapped. "You have done an acceptable job of sleuthing, I won't deny that, but your job here is finished now and I'll thank you to permit me to deal with my nephew as I see fit. And to remove yourself and your associate from my house forthwith."

Whit frowned at him, though he kept silent; it was plain that he did not care one bit for Joshua Brandywine or the man's pompous, imperious ways. Sabina felt the same. It was not in her nature to make this fact known to him, as John might well have done if he were here, but neither did she have to meekly suffer his insolence.

"Gladly," she said, "once you have made out a check payable to Carpenter and Quincannon, Professional Detective Services."

"A check will be mailed to you in due course—"

"I prefer to have it now. In full payment of the balance of the agreed-upon fee, plus an additional five hundred dollars."

"Eh? Another five hundred?"

"The amount of the bonus you promised if the solution was achieved within forty-eight hours. According to my calculations, it has been approximately forty-two hours since you first retained my services."

"A temporary whim on my part. No such promise was put in writing—"

Whit stepped forward. "You heard Mrs. Carpenter," he said in a not quite threatening voice. "A check in the full amount including the bonus and then we'll leave."

Brandywine, hemming, hawing, and sputtering, produced and peered at his gold watch, as if to verify the all too obvious claim. Sabina seized the opportunity to offer an appropriate goad.

"Make haste, Mr. Brandywine," she said. "Tempus fidgets."

17

SABINA

It was early afternoon by the time she deposited Joshua Brandywine's check in the agency account at the Miner's Bank, paid Whit for his service, stopped in at the Western Union office, and returned to the offices of Carpenter and Quincannon, Professional Detective Services. There had been no further wires regarding Jeffrey Gaunt or his sister—or any concerning the Delford matter—nor had any messages pertaining to Gaunt been slipped through the mail slot in the office door.

The outcome of the Brandywine affair had been quite satisfying, the more so because it had presented her with the sort of knotty problem John took considerable pride in addressing, and she had resolved it with dispatch and earned a substantial fee. Few enough of their cases could be marked closed in less than forty-eight hours. He took delight in recounting the details of his triumphs; she looked forward to regaling him with hers, though with considerably less bombast, when he returned.

It was axiomatic in their business that there were periods when they were besieged with investigative work and periods when there was little or none. This summer thus far was proving to be one of the fertile stretches. The Grass Valley case, the felonious rainmakers in the San Joaquin Valley, the Brandywine conundrum, and now two more prospective clients via the afternoon mail. Well, just one, actually: a consultation request from Jackson Pollard, chief claims adjuster at Great Western Insurance, regarding a suspected fraudulent injury claim. They had done a number of jobs for Pollard and Great Western, the most notable of which was the Bughouse Affair last year—their introduction to the shrewdly daft Charles the Third, who in his Sherlock Holmes guise had been as responsible as she and John for bringing three interrelated cases to successful conclusions.

The second letter, written in a spidery and rather shaky hand, was from a woman who signed herself Miss Lucretia L. Moffit. Carpenter and Quincannon, Professional Detective Services, received its share of oddball inquiries, some amusing, some disconcerting, some—like this one—rather pathetic. It seemed Miss Moffit was being plagued by a serial prowler who had slipped into her home on at least three separate occasions in the middle of the night. But he was no ordinary prowler, she wrote; instead of stealing items from her substantial collection of buttonhooks, thimbles, and other sewing-related material, he brought in and left more of each. As a result she now had almost twice as many as before. She had no idea why anyone would do such a thing. The police refused to believe her; could Mrs. Carpenter or Mr. Quincannon track down the culprit and put an end to this outrage?

Sabina sighed. A dotty old lady likely starved for attention. In the kindest terms possible she penned a reply to Miss Moffit stating that previous commitments made it impossible for them to undertake an investigation on her behalf. She added her sincere hope that the intruder would soon tire of his nocturnal trespasses and bring no more unwanted gifts.

When the letter was finished, she reread Jackson Pollard's missive. There was a certain urgency in the injury claim, he'd written, so if they were available, a consultation at their earliest convenience was required. Sabina cranked the handle on the wall telephone, gave the Exchange operator the number of Great Western Insurance. It took five minutes for a connection to be made, as sometimes happened with Mr. Alexander Graham Bell's invention, still in its infancy. She spoke to Pollard's secretary; he had already left for the day, but he had left word that he would be in his office until noon tomorrow. She scheduled a meeting with him for ten o'clock. If John had yet to return by then, she would keep the appointment herself.

She wondered what the situation was in Delford. Obviously it had taken longer than he'd anticipated to expose and arrest Leopold Saxe and his cohorts. Whatever the reason for the delay, he wouldn't remain there a minute longer than absolutely necessary. If he returned on this afternoon's train, there would be little enough if any time for a lengthy discussion. In order to attend tonight's supper meeting at the offices of Voting Rights for Women, she would have to leave the agency no later than four-thirty. Home first to feed Adam and Eve and change clothes, then an early arrival at VRW so as to spend time with Amity before the meal and the speeches by the Southern California suffragist delegates.

Thought of food produced hunger pangs, which in turn prodded her out of the office. All she had eaten today was two slices of bread with black currant jam for breakfast, hardly enough to satisfy her until supper. After posting the letter to Miss Lucretia L. Moffit, she crossed the street to Sullivan's Fish Market. Usually she did her seafood shopping at Tony's Fish Stand in the open-air California Market, San Francisco's "entrepôt of foods," which took up an entire block from Pine to California Streets between Montgomery and Kearney. But there was no time for a trip there today. She would have to make do with Sullivan's somewhat inferior selection.

She bought two pieces of fresh cod, the cats' favorite, and for herself a large crab and shrimp cocktail. These she took back to the office, along with a fresh-baked soft pretzel supplied by one of the sidewalk food vendors outside the market. She seldom ate at her desk—never, when John was present—but time constraints made it necessary today.

For the remainder of her time in the office she entered the sum received from Joshua Brandywine in the agency's financial ledger, along with a notation of the amount paid to Whit Slattery for his services, then wrote a report of her investigation for their files. No messengers or other visitors appeared, nor had John when the hands on the Seth Thomas clock reached four-thirty. Either circumstances had forced him to spend another day in Delford, or the Southern Pacific train from the San Joaquin Valley was late arriving. Should it be the latter, he would come straight to the agency. In case he did, she wrote a brief note to let him know all was well and explaining why she was departing early, and placed it on his desk blotter.

She was fortunate to board a trolley for Russian Hill just as it was about to leave the Market Street station, which gave her a few extra minutes at home to prepare for the evening ahead. Adam and Eve made short work of the cod she'd bought and yowled for more while she changed clothes. She took her time choosing her supper wear, finally settling on a high-necked, floor-length beige dress with leg-o'-mutton sleeves. A beaded purse and a fashionable ivory velvet cartwheel plumed hat completed her ensemble.

The headquarters of Voting Rights for Women was located on Parrot Street. Sabina arrived twenty-five minutes early, which allowed her sufficient time to meet the honored guests and to have a brief private conversation with Amity. Her friend was more than welcoming, the period of awkwardness between them now a thing of the past; they arranged a resumption of their bicycling in Golden Gate Park on Sunday morning.

She had a splendid time at the supper. The food, catered by Amity and another wealthy member of the movement, was plentiful and well prepared; Sabina tucked into it with what Callie termed "delicate gusto." The speeches by the Southern California delegates were spirited and uplifting, though their absolute certainty that the voting rights amendment would pass in the November election struck Sabina as a shade too optimistic. The mostly male opposition to its passage was also well organized, better funded, and unequivocal in its determination to defeat the measure.

Ten o'clock had come and gone when she left the VRW headquarters. Rather than wait in the hope of hailing a passing hansom to take her home, she boarded a nearby trolley car. This neighborhood was a relatively safe one, as was her own, but it was not always safe for a woman to travel alone on public conveyances at this hour. No one bothered her, however, on the car or when she alighted at her stop half a block from her building.

Streetlights illuminated the otherwise empty sidewalk as she trudged uphill. It was so quiet at this hour she could hear the heels of her Cromwell high-button shoes clicking softly on the pavement. A single-horse brougham, its side lamps dark, its outside driver's seat empty, was parked in the shadow of an acacia tree at the curb in front. She took less notice of it as she passed by than she should have.

Just as she turned onto the path that led to the porch steps, the creaking sound of someone alighting from the brougham came from behind her. Quick footsteps and a familiar medicinal whiff warned her of the presence of danger. She started to pivot around, to reach into her bag for the Remington derringer—too late.

An arm snaked around her neck, bent her backward, and pinned her against a braced, hard-muscled body. Before she could free the derringer, or make any sort of outcry, a wet cloth slapped over her nose and mouth, its potent reek causing her to gasp and then gag.

Ether!

The voice that said harshly in her ear, "I've been waiting for you, Mrs. Carpenter," belonged to Jeffrey Gaunt.

She struggled desperately, trying and failing to claw the cloth away so she could breathe, to pull loose of his grasp by kicking at his shins. Her senses reeled from the ether; her strength swiftly ebbed. Waves of dizziness overcame her.

Her last memory was of being dragged backward into the darkened brougham.

18

QUINCANNON

The reply to his Chicago wire had finally come through when Quincannon stopped again at the telegraph office at nine-thirty Saturday morning, on his way back from a brief visit with the railroad station agent and a private consultation with Marshal Tom Boxhardt. The answers to his questions were all just as he had expected. Now he had all the necessary information he needed to support his deductions.

Two drawbacks prevented him from fully relishing what was about to take place. The delay in receiving the wire was one; the fact that Sheriff Beadle and his deputies still had yet to arrive from Fresno was the other. These annoyances made it all but impossible for him to be finished with business in time to board the day's one Stockton–San Francisco passenger train when it passed through Delford.

He crossed the street to the bank to collect Aram Kasabian.

"An unveiling is about to take place at the jail," he said, "that you and Mayor Parnell will want to witness."

"What unveiling? I thought that with the two fugitives and O. H. Goodland in custody awaiting Sheriff Beadle's arrival, everything about the recent unpleasantness was settled."

"Not quite yet, though it soon will be," Quincannon said. "I'll explain in full once all parties are gathered in the marshal's office."

He made a similar statement to James Parnell at the mayor's mercantile store, after which the three of them went to the hotel where Cora Lee Johnson was being held under guard. When the deputy on duty unlocked her door, they found her dressed once again in the green-and-blue outfit she'd worn at the mortar launching. She was as sullen as the night before, and except for another angry claim of innocence, uncommunicative. The party then proceeded to the jail.

The marshal's office and the two adjoining prisoner cells were all housed in the same large room. Mortimer Rollins and O. H. Goodland were glowering and glaring at each other through the bars between their respective cells. The party's entrance turned their attention, brought them to their cell doors. Quincannon and the others spread out in a ragged half circle between them and a pair of cluttered desks.

Boxhardt said wearily, "They've been jawing for the past hour, throwing accusations back and forth."

The wheat farmer was in a barely controlled rage, exacerbated by a blotchy skinned hangover. He growled, "You can't keep me locked up in here, dammit. Get me Sam Haskins like I been asking you to."

"Mr. Quincannon says you won't be needing a lawyer."

"No? Then let me out."

"In good time."

Goodland appealed to Parnell. "James? You're the mayor, make Tom set me loose right now."

"Mrs. Daks and myself as well," Rollins said before Parnell could answer. "This is all an intolerable misunderstanding. We are legitimate pluviculturists—obviously the victims of mistaken identity. We have committed no crimes in the Midwest or in Delford." His voice trembled with injured innocence and righteous indignation. Bluff and bluster to the very end.

"You tried to make off in the middle of the night with the coalition's two thousand dollars," Boxhardt reminded him.

"I've told you and told you. We had no idea the money was hidden on the wagon trace."

Quincannon said, "Fraud and theft are the least of your crimes in this community."

"Now what are you accusing us of?"

"Willful homicide."

The pronouncement caused a stir of surprise.

"You can't mean the murder of poor Leonide," Rollins said. "The man who shot him is right here in the cell next to mine."

"That's a damn lie!" Goodland shouted. "I didn't kill that phony rainmaker and you and that woman there know it!"

"Of course you did. No one else could have."

"Liar!"

"That he is," Quincannon agreed. "Mr. Goodland did no shooting last night."

"By God," the wheat farmer said, "it's about time somebody believed me."

Rollins caught hold of the bars of his cell and poked his face between them. "How can you make such a statement?" he demanded of Quincannon. "You were at the shack, you know what happened as well as I do. Goodland and Leonide were together inside. I repeat: no one else could have done it."

"But someone else did. You, Rollins."

"My name is not Rollins—"

"Mortimer Rollins. Confidence man, thief, murderer."

"You must have taken leave of your senses. I was outside with you when the shot was fired. How could I possibly be guilty?"

"By means of clever planning, careful timing, and the help of your accomplice. Or rather, your paramour."

Cora Lee roused herself and said scornfully, "I suppose you mean me. A ridiculous accusation."

"No more ridiculous than the fact that your real name is Cora Lee Johnson and you were not the wife of the dead man, true name Leopold Saxe, but his paramour as well."

Kasabian asked, "But if they conspired to kill Saxe, what was their motive?"

"Revenge. Lust. Greed."

"Revenge?"

"Saxe was a womanizer. I suspect Cora Lee had had enough of his illicit affairs and out of spite took his partner as her lover. His advances to Mr. Goodland's daughter, successful or not, were the final straw."

"Preposterous!" Rollins cried. "Nefarious!"

"Fact," Quincannon said. "As for your motives, you'd grown to hate Saxe for a different reason. He'd taken over control of your swindles, reduced you to a subservient role by the force of his will. With him dead, you could have Cora Lee and the money stolen from the coalition, and be your own master again."

"Utter rot, I say."

"Mr. Goodland's rash behavior two days ago gave you the perfect foil for your scheme. And the scheme itself worked smoothly enough. If I hadn't come to Delford, you might well have gotten away with it."

"What scheme?" Parnell said. "How did they work it?"

This was the moment Quincannon had been waiting for. He drew it out by producing his already charged pipe, setting a match flame to it, and puffing until he had a good draw. He fancied he could feel the crackling of suspense among the gathered.

"Well, sir? How *did* they work it?"

Quincannon exhaled a haze of smoke. Instead of answering the mayor directly, he turned to Cora Lee and asked, "Why did you fire the mortar last night?"

The question caught her off guard. "Why . . . I was the only person on the platform. Leonide and Ben were inside the shack with Goodland."

"Why didn't you wait for them to come out?"

"The launching was scheduled for seven. Rather than delay, I went ahead on my own."

"But you'd never fired the mortar before."

"Not here, but elsewhere—"

"Nowhere else. Your frightened actions after lighting the fuse prove last night was your first time and that it was done by prearrangement. Rollins loaded the mortar while I was talking to Saxe so it would be ready for you. Properly loading such a device is more difficult and dangerous than firing it."

Quincannon shifted his gaze to O. H. Goodland. "Mr. Goodland, why did you go to the shack after being warned to stay away?"

"A message was slipped under the door of my room. Asking me to come there promptly at seven to settle our differences and signed with Daks' name. The word 'promptly' was underlined."

"Leonide did write such a note," Cora Lee lied. "He told me he had, which is why I wasn't concerned when I saw Goodland arrive."

"No, the note was written by you or Rollins—a careful forgery."

She started to deny it, changed her mind, and said nothing.

Quincannon produced the Colt New Pocket revolver, which Boxhardt had let him have earlier. He showed it to the wheat farmer. "Did you take this weapon with you last night, Mr. Goodland?"

"I did not. I had no weapon when I went to the shack and Daks had no idea what I was doing there. He was telling me that when somebody—this bird Rollins—clubbed me from behind."

"When did you last have the gun in your possession?"

"Friday afternoon, after I made the mistake of threatening Daks or Saxe with it. The marshal took it away from me."

Boxhardt said, "I emptied it and put it in his saddlebag at the hotel livery. Rollins was there at the time; he must've seen me do it, and come back later and swiped it."

"That he did."

"I won't stand for any more of this calumny." Rollins' voice had risen. He had finally begun to lose his composure. "How dare you accuse me when you know it's impossible for me to be guilty of shooting Leonide. I'll say it again: I was outside when he was killed. You saw me, Marshal. And you, Quincannon, you heard him beg for his life and you heard the fatal shot. You can't deny the truth of that."

"I can't and won't deny what I *seemed* to hear."

"Seemed? What do you mean, seemed?"

Quincannon removed another object from his pocket. "I found this on the floor shortly after we broke into the shack. When I picked it up it was hot to the touch."

They all looked at the shell casing displayed in the upturned palm of his hand.

"Couldn't have come from Mr. Goodland's gun," Boxhardt said. "Revolvers don't eject spent shells. Only one bullet was fired from that Colt's, and the empty was in the cylinder."

Kasabian asked, "Then where did that one come from?"

"The fire inside the boiler," Quincannon said, "where Rollins placed it after he clubbed Mr. Goodland, shot Saxe, and put the revolver in Mr. Goodland's hand. A blank cartridge. The heat exploded the powder, simulating a gunshot, and the explosion kicked the casing out through the open fire door. Rollins had used the trick before—I'll explain where and how shortly—and so he was able to gauge within a minute or so when it would go off."

"So that's what happened, and with me as the goat." Goodland glared sideways at Rollins, reached a hand through into the other's cell. "By Christ, if these bars weren't between us—"

Rollins quickly backed away.

"The shot that actually killed Saxe," Boxhardt said. "How was that done?"

"Fired when Cora Lee launched the rocket when she saw Mr. Goodland arrive promptly at seven. The boom of the mortar drowned the sound of the report. Timing, you see?"

"But what about the locked door?"

"It wasn't locked. Rollins created the illusion that it was locked by gripping the knob and rattling it while he blocked the doorway with his body. The bolt wasn't damaged, a fact that was overlooked in the excitement."

"By everyone except you."

"The eyes of a trained detective," Quincannon said.

Rollins had to know he was caught, but in desperation he played his last card. "Leonide was still alive when we were all outside. You know he was, you heard him beg for his life—you and the others heard him!"

"No," Quincannon said, "we didn't."

Once again he paused dramatically and then asked the banker, "Mr. Kasabian, do you remember my telling you that Saxe and Rollins were once variety performers in Chicago?"

"Yes. Low comedy and specialty acts, you said."

"I didn't know for certain what the specialty acts were until a short while ago, when I received a wire from the Chicago office of the Pinkerton agency. One act the pair performed was a magic show in which a pistol was supposedly fired on command. Saxe was the magician, Rollins the one who invented and staged the trick. Rollins was also a performer with his own specialty. One he performed quite well, by all accounts."

"What specialty, for heaven's sake?"

Quincannon said, "Ventriloquism."

Sheriff Beadle and his deputies finally rattled into Delford aboard a prison wagon, anticlimactically, a few minutes shy of noon. By this time, even though Rollins once more lapsed into churlish silence, Cora Lee Johnson had admitted her part in the murder scheme. She claimed the entire plan had been Rollins' and that he had coerced her into going along with it—a falsehood, to be sure, but one she had already begun to play well with lamentations and tears of bogus remorse. She was a comely woman; Quincannon had little doubt that she would be able to convince a male jury to be lenient.

Ordinarily he would have basked in the approbation heaped upon him by his client, the marshal, the mayor, O. H. Goodland, and Sheriff A. Beadle, but now that the case had been resolved, Sabina's welfare was uppermost in his mind and he was anxious to return to San Francisco. Even though he'd missed the daily passenger train, another night in Delford would have been intolerable. With the assistance of Parnell and Boxhardt, he arranged with the station agent for the special privilege of departing on the next train through Delford, a slow freight leaving at three o'clock. According to the

Southern Pacific timetable, the freight would put him in Stockton in time to catch the evening passenger train westbound from Sacramento. If the latter were on schedule, he would arrive back in the city at eight-thirty.

The one thing he made sure to do before departing Delford was to collect the balance of his fee from Aram Kasabian. The banker insisted on paying him in cash rather than by check, which was fine with Quincannon. There was nothing so comforting as the feel of crisp new greenbacks. Nothing, that was, except for the feel of Sabina in his arms.

19

QUINCANNON

Frustration dogged him on the return trip. The slow freight ran nearly half an hour late leaving Delford, and the delay might well have caused him to miss the westbound passenger train except that it, too, was running late—more than an hour late by the time it reached Stockton. And for one reason or another, the blasted rattler was yet another twenty-five minutes behind schedule when it chuffed into the Third and Townsend depot. A pox on Southern Pacific! He would write them a letter of complaint, not that it was likely to have any positive effect.

His Hampden stem-winder gave the time as 10:15 when he climbed into one of the waiting cabs. Too late to go calling on Sabina tonight. He'd struggled with the decision, but as much as he wanted to satisfy himself that all was well with her, it would take half an hour to reach her flat and she might be in bed asleep by the time he got there. She would not take kindly to receiving him at such a late hour, particularly in his tired, rumpled, sweat-dampened, and rather malodorous condition. The slow freight had been loaded with cattle, and the caboose, in which he'd ridden with the brakeman, anything but spotlessly maintained.

He gave the driver his home address on Leavenworth.

As tired as he was, he slept a full eight hours. After coffee and a light breakfast, he rode a trolley to Russian Hill. Sabina didn't answer her bell. Well, that was nothing to be concerned about. She might have gone to church, or to visit Callie French, or resumed her Sunday bicycle outings with Amity Wellman in Golden Gate Park.

Another trolley took him downtown to Market Street. When he entered the agency, he found a scatter of mail on the floor under the door slot—Saturday's delivery. It would not have been there if Sabina had come into the office yesterday. Not that it was unusual that she hadn't; only the press of business brought her in on Saturdays. A brief, undated note on his desk blotter, anticipating his return with the statement that she was closing up half an hour early in order to attend a Voting Rights for Women supper, must have been written late Friday afternoon.

No cause for alarm in any of that, but there was cause, by God, in three other items he discovered.

The first was among the mail, a hand-delivered envelope addressed to Sabina. Under the letterhead of James Pollard, Great Western Insurance's chief claims adjuster, and bearing yesterday's date, were a dozen lines taking her to task for failing to keep their ten o'clock appointment. He had attempted to telephone her and then waited in his office until noon, he wrote, and unless she presented him with an acceptable excuse first thing Monday morning, he would give the injury claim to another investigative agency.

Sabina was punctual to a fault. And Quincannon had never known her not to give notification if circumstances prevented her from keeping an appointment with a client, especially a regular one such as Pollard.

He hardly ever snooped in her desk, but Pollard's missive drove him to it. That was where he found the two wires, in a bottom drawer beneath a report of a two-day investigation she had successfully conducted while he was away. The first wire, from Pinkerton's New Orleans office detailing the suspected crimes of Jeffrey Gaunt and Lady One-Eye, was disturbing enough. The date on it indicated it had been delivered before his departure for Delford. Why hadn't she shown it to him? To spare him what she felt was undue concern?

The second wire, from Sheriff Hezekiah Thorpe informing them of Lady One-Eye's imminent trial date and Gaunt's sudden disappearance, must have arrived while he was in Delford and increased his anxiety twofold. "Whereabouts unknown"—an ominous phrase. Where else would that blackguard have gone but here to San Francisco?

Dark thoughts tumbled through Quincannon's mind. If Gaunt harmed a hair on Sabina's head—!

Steady now, he told himself, don't go off half-cocked. She's all right, Gaunt hasn't done anything to her yet. Find her, make sure she's safe. Then track him down and neutralize his threat one way or another.

Rather than continuing to rely on public transportation, he

went to the United Carriage Company office outside the Palace Hotel, where he arranged to rent a small hooded buggy and a good horse—damn the expense. A cab delivered him to the company's stables on Eighth Street where he claimed the equipage. From there he drove back to the foot of Russian Hill.

Sabina still had not returned. He rang the bell of the other flat in the building, in the hope that one or both of the occupants, a young married couple named Christopher, had seen her recently. As blasted luck would have it, they were also away.

He drove to Hyde Street, where Elizabeth Petrie resided. The former police matron was home, but she had nothing to tell him. She hadn't had any contact with Sabina other than a brief telephone conversation shortly after their return from Grass Valley.

Callie and Hugh French's home on Van Ness Avenue drew him next. Sabina's cousin, dressed in Sunday lounging clothes, greeted him effusively. Through a smile that felt pasted on, he told her he had just returned from a three-day business trip to the San Joaquin Valley and was eager to confer with Sabina. She wasn't at her flat; had Callie seen her today?

"No, not since our luncheon on Thursday," she said. Then, with keen perception, "You seem worried, John. Is everything all right?"

"Worried? No, not about Sabina," he lied. "I'm just eager to see her. Have you any idea where she might be?"

"None, I'm afraid."

"She didn't indicate any plans for the weekend when you lunched with her?"

"No. John . . . are you sure there's no cause for concern?"

"Not in the way you mean. You needn't worry."

"Well, if you say so. But your and dear Sabina's profession frightens me sometimes. After what happened to her late husband and all the dangers you and she have faced together . . ."

Callie's fretting only served to increase his anxiety. He patted her hand, said something mundanely reassuring, and made a hasty exit.

Amity Wellman and her husband, a well-known dealer in Spanish antiques, resided on Telegraph Hill. Quincannon went there next. Kamiko, the Wellmans' adopted Japanese daughter, answered his ring and his questions. Mrs. Wellman was not at home, she had gone bicycling in Golden Gate Park, as was her custom on Sundays. Yes, she had mentioned having seen Mrs. Carpenter on Friday evening, at the Voting Rights for Women supper, and that they had arranged to ride together today.

This relieved him, but only until he reached the Golden Gate Ladies Bicycle Club on Clayton Street near the Panhandle. The woman on duty there knew Sabina, but said she hadn't appeared today as expected; Mrs. Wellman had waited half an hour for her before riding off to join the other members of the club.

Tense, frustrated, Quincannon waited nearly an hour for Amity Wellman's return, sitting in the rented buggy and smoking pipeful after pipeful of shag cut until his mouth and throat were scorched raw. Mrs. Wellman, a slender, handsome woman with hair the color of taffy, was surprised to see him since they had never met in person before. She expressed dismay at Sabina's failure to keep their date; Sabina had been enthusiastic about resuming their Sunday rides together, she said, and in good spirits when they parted after the Friday-night supper.

"There must be a good reason why she didn't come today," Mrs. Wellman said. "An urgent business matter that came up suddenly, perhaps."

Quincannon recalled the report he'd found in her desk of her recent two-day investigation. He'd only glanced through it, but he recognized the prominent client's name, Joshua Brandywine, and remembered the man's address on Nob Hill. Could something related to that case have required an urgent follow-up on Sabina's part? A slim possibility, since she had marked it "Closed," but he had no other leads to check.

The menswear magnate was home, but he refused an audience with Quincannon. He sent word by way of a dour-faced housekeeper that he hadn't seen Mrs. Carpenter since Friday morning, and furthermore wanted nothing more to do with her or Carpenter and Quincannon, Professional Detective Services. Whatever had happened to ruffle Brandywine's feathers couldn't have been Sabina's doing; she took pains to be civil with clients, and if there had been a contretemps of any import she would have mentioned it in her report. Dead end. The Brandywine case had nothing to do with her disappearance.

Evening was coming on now. With nowhere else to go, he drove once more to Russian Hill. Ringing Sabina's bell proved as futile as the previous two times. So did another attempt to summon the Christophers.

Desperation led him to do then what he would never have

done under normal circumstances: invade the sanctity of her home. If Gaunt was not responsible for her absence and she learned of his intrusion, she might never forgive him. But he had to know if everything was as it should be inside her flat. There might even be something there that would explain her failure to keep the appointment with Amity Wellman.

The lock on her door was not as easy to pick as most, but he'd expected this: she was as security conscious as he. Quincannon had to work at it for several minutes before the tumblers finally released. He stepped quickly inside, to be greeted by a pair of mewling cats. He cudgeled his memory for their names . . . Adam and Eve. This was the first time he had seen either of them, never yet having been invited inside Sabina's private domain. On all their social outings to date, she had greeted him at the door and parted from him afterward on the front porch.

He made a swift check of each of the flat's four rooms. That all were empty and showed no signs of disorder was a temporary relief, tempered by the flat's faintly musty odor and then ended by the cats' behavior. They kept following him, mewling loudly all the while—cries of hunger, he realized, when he saw their licked-clean food bowls in the kitchen. How long since they'd been fed? At least a day, likely two or more. Sabina would never have abandoned them without making arrangements for feeding, no matter how urgent a new investigation that might have come her way.

The sense of dread seized him again. Something had happened to her, Friday night or early Saturday. There could be little doubt of it now.

Gaunt. Accosted by that goddamned rogue somewhere in the city. But he hadn't silenced her, not yet. She was alive, she *had* to be. He refused to think otherwise.

Adam's and Eve's cries grated on Quincannon's nerves. He found a bottle of milk and a package of liver in the icebox, filled their bowls to the brim. Then he commenced a search, looking for anything that might give him a clue to what had happened to her.

A Wooton secretary-desk in the parlor yielded nothing except private papers. In different circumstances he would have been reassured of his position in her affections by the fact that none of the letters she'd kept bore a man's signature; now, he barely noticed. There was nothing in any of the other rooms, either.

Quincannon reset the door lock when he left the flat, hurried downstairs. When he emerged onto the porch, he encountered the Christophers, Everett and Letitia, just returning from their day's outing. He assumed a neutral expression as they met at the foot of the steps.

"Mrs. Carpenter isn't home," he said, "and I very much need to speak with her. Would you have any idea where she might be?"

Plump, dark-haired Letitia Christopher said, "I'm sorry, no. We've been away all day visiting my mother in Oakland."

"When did you last see Mrs. Carpenter?"

"Well . . . I'm not quite sure."

"At any time yesterday?"

"No. It must be, oh, three days."

"At least that," her husband said.

"Did you happen to notice if her lamps were lighted last night or Friday night?"

They hadn't. Good neighbors, the sort that tended to their own affairs and respected the privacy of others. Hell, damn, and blast!

Quincannon bid them good evening, climbed into the rented buggy. And sat there, his large hands gripping the reins almost as tightly as he would have gripped Jeffrey Gaunt's neck.

What now? Maintaining a passive vigil here was out of the question. Even if he'd had the patience for it, it would surely prove futile. Sabina was not going to come to him under her own power, not tonight, not at any time in the foreseeable future. He had to find her. And to do that, he had to find Gaunt. How to accomplish it, where to begin? Formidable task in a city this size, one that seemed insurmountable.

But it wasn't—he wouldn't let it be.

She had to be somewhere.

Where?

20

SABINA

At first she'd had no idea where she was imprisoned. Now she did, after two long, miserable days and a third just beginning, but the knowledge did her no good. She still had not found a possible means of escape.

She had run a gamut of emotions during that interminable period. Disorientation when she'd awakened on a filthy cot after God only knew how many hours of unconsciousness, her head aching abominably, her mouth dry and her throat parched—the aftereffects of the ether. Confusion when her vision cleared enough to penetrate the gloom of her surroundings. Bewilderment that she had been brought to a place like this and left here alone. Fear that she had overcome and continued to hold at bay by sheer force of will. Disgust at herself for not paying closer heed to John's concerns, the lapse in caution that had allowed Jeffrey Gaunt to catch her as he had. Anger at him that had grown into an alternately hot and cold, sustaining fury.

Except for the ether, he hadn't abused her in any other way. Her body bore no marks or wounds, and her clothing was intact, hardly disarrayed at all, when she awakened. And there had been no sign of him since; he had left her completely alone in this place with no food, no water, not even a blanket to help take away the night's chill.

He had locked her in here to die.

Why, instead of simply doing away with her by gunshot or some other lethal means? Initially she'd thought that he might be squeamish about killing a woman in a direct confrontation, and so by employing this method he avoided blood on his hands. Now she was convinced that the kidnapping and imprisonment were by coldly calculated design. His pose as a Southern gentleman disguised his true nature—a sadistic shell of a man lacking all human feeling other than his warped protective love for his sister.

If Sabina simply disappeared, foul play could not be proven against him. And when she failed to appear to give her damning testimony at Lady One-Eye's trial, the chances of acquittal would increase considerably. He would then have his revenge and his sister's freedom, both. And once again he would get away with cold-blooded murder, damn his black soul, for there could be little doubt now that he was responsible for the deaths of the gambler in New Orleans and the landowner in San Antonio.

One other emotion had been born of this understanding—an unwavering determination not to let his plan succeed. She would not die in this foul place. She would not. *She would not.*

And foul it was, literally. Cold, damp, dirty, rife with an

array of rank odors that she had identified one by one: salt water, rotting wood, dust, paint, linseed oil, turpentine, rodent and bird droppings. Rife with sounds, too: the creaks and groans of old wood, the lapping of water close by outside, the chittering and scurrying of rats. Sabina had seen some of them, red-eyed shadows flitting through the daytime gloom.

The long nights were the worst. She lay wrapped cocoon-like in her evening cape, sleeping only fitfully for short periods before some sound brought her awake. Her loathing for rats was not as intense as in many women, those who would cower and swoon at the mere thought of a rodent large or small, but when she heard the creatures moving in the thick darkness she couldn't help imagining that they were about to pounce on her, tear into her flesh with their sharp teeth and claws.

Rationally she knew this would not happen—not yet. Despite more than two days without food and water, she had lost little of her strength. Whenever one of the rats seemed to venture too close, she hammered the floor with the length of rusty pipe she'd found to frighten it away. But if she remained trapped here another two, three, four days, the rats would sense her weakening condition and eventually they would attack.

Hunger was bad enough, painfully cramping her empty stomach, but thirst was worse by far. Her mouth and throat were so arid this morning she had difficulty swallowing. And the dampness and sinus-clogging dust made breathing painful.

As on the previous two mornings, it had been the moans of foghorns mounted on buoys in the bay and the shrieks of seagulls that had awakened her. She lay shivering until a paroxysm of dry coughing prodded her into a sitting position. When it subsided she stood, adjusted her now filthy cape with cracked and blistered fingers, then spent a little time flexing her arms and legs to free them of stiffness.

She could see well enough again now that the night had ended. There was a ragged, foot-wide hole in the roof—possibly created or enlarged by the small marsh birds nesting in the rafters, or by gulls trying to get at eggs in the nest—that admitted a funnel of daylight. And a score of thin threads and ribbons of gray daylight came through chinks in the warped wooden walls. Heavy shadows still crouched in corners and among the rafters, shrouded the contents of the cavernous building.

Her explorations had identified it for her. It was or had been a repair shop for boats, the rear half of the warehouse section built on pilings. An isolated derelict situated at the edge of the bay—the salt smell that permeated the structure and the lapping of wavelets beneath the floorboards told her that—but just where she couldn't be sure.

How had Gaunt found it? He hadn't been in San Francisco long enough to go scouting in unfamiliar territory. Or was it unfamiliar to him? Had he been here before in his travels? Unlikely, given the information the Pinkertons had provided on his past activities; Sacramento and Grass Valley must be the farthest west he'd ventured until this past week.

He must know someone in San Francisco, then, someone who had told him of this derelict shop and supplied him with keys. Sabina couldn't imagine who, but it didn't really matter now. Any more than it mattered where Gaunt had gone after depositing her here, whether or not he was still somewhere in the city. Unless he came to check on her, make sure she hadn't escaped. If he did, she thought with a fresh surge of fury, he would find a pipe-wielding hellcat waiting for him.

But he wouldn't. As far as he was concerned, this prison was escapeproof. And so far he was right.

If there were any other buildings nearby, they were untenanted. She had yelled herself hoarse, beat on the walls and corrugated iron doors with the length of pipe and other implements. There was no sense in trying again today—it would be a hopeless waste of time, energy, breath. Gaunt would not have confined her within shouting, noise-making distance of anyone who might hear and come to her rescue.

No one would come to her rescue. Not John, who must know by now that she was missing and that Gaunt was responsible. He would be frantic, trust in the hope that she was still alive, do everything in his power to find her—but how could he, when she herself didn't know exactly where she was?

No, her only chance of survival lay in escape. Two days now, and she'd been over every inch of space half a dozen times without finding a way out or anything she could use to create one. But hope remained strong in her. There had to be some means of escape.

The cot was in what must have been the repair business's office, walled off by plywood at the inner end of the building. There was nothing else in it except for a rickety desk, a broken chair, and a scattering of debris. The entrance to it was doorless.

Two sets of double doors, both of rusty corrugated iron,

gave access to the building, one set next to the makeshift office, the other at the bayside end that Sabina judged would open onto some sort of pier. Both were tightly secured with padlocks. She knew that because the padlock on the bayside doors was on the inside, heavy and thick-stapled, and because no matter how long and hard she rattled and banged and pried at the other set, she failed to part them so much as an inch.

The hole in the roof was up near the peak; there was no possible way for her to climb up to it. The walls and floor were in warped condition, but the chinks that admitted daylight were too small to admit any tool larger than a screwdriver. If any such tools had been abandoned here, Gaunt had anticipated their use and disposed of them. The piece of pipe was the only object she'd found of any possible use, which thus far had been limited to frightening off the rats. The palms of both her hands were lacerated from vain attempts to batter loose wall boards and floorboards.

Another series of mournful wails from the foghorns, followed a few seconds later by the blast of a ship's horn, goaded her into motion. She groped her way out of the office, into the center of the slightly down-slanted warehouse where she stood peering around, reorienting herself.

There was little enough to see in the gloom. Overhead, lengths of oxidized chain hung from a winchlike contraption strung across the beams, too high up for her to reach. The floor was strewn with various pieces of board lumber, a broken sheet of plywood, a coil of heavy rope so decayed the hemp fibers had crumbled when she tried to pick it up, the skeleton of a rowboat laid askew on a pair of sawhorses. She had examined the skeleton and the sawhorses, one of which had a fractured leg, with the thought of making some use of their bones, but she hadn't sufficient strength, even with the pipe as a lever, to rip the loose, splintered ones free. Even if she'd succeeded, she knew now that the chunks would have been as useless to her as the rest of the scattered lumber.

A rusted metal drainage trough some eight inches wide extended down along the side wall. Shallow, empty except for rat droppings and dead insects and dust, it led to an opening in the bayside wall next to one of the corrugated door halves. The opening had been clogged with debris that she'd cleared out. Prying and chipping at the hole with the pipe had splintered off enough decayed wood to enlarge it slightly, but the vertical boards on both sides were thick and firmly nailed in place.

The gurgling of the bay water around the pilings beneath was a painful reminder of her thirst. Biting her lip, she commanded herself once again to ignore physical discomfort, focus on the task at hand. In slow shuffling steps she began to prowl through the gloom, feeling along the walls for any loose board she might have missed previously. There were none. Again she made a futile effort to create separation between the bayside doors. Again she scuffed over the length and width of the enclosure, avoiding the shadowy obstacles . . . no loose boards there, either, no overlooked tool or other useful object.

At the front set of doors she lost her composure for a moment, beat on them furiously with the pipe until the palm of her hand was slick with blood. A scream born of frustration welled in the back of her throat; it took an effort of will to keep it from bursting forth. If she were to give in to such an impulse, she might not be able to stop.

Slowly again she made her way back along the side wall where the drainage trough was. When she stepped up close to it, the toe of her shoe stubbed on an uptilted edge, causing her to stumble off balance, to drop the blood-slick pipe when she threw her hands out to brace herself against the wall. The pipe clattered into the trough, setting up ringing echoes that disturbed the nesting birds and sent one of them flying out through the roof hole. A gull loosed a raucous cry somewhere nearby.

She bent to fumble for the pipe, found it, and when she straightened, her toe again struck the protruding edge. In a kind of furious retaliation she kicked at it. The metal shivered, rattled at the impact.

She started to move ahead. And then stopped and stood still.

The trough, she thought.

The trough?

21

QUINCANNON

After leaving Russian Hill Sunday evening, he had driven to the Hall of Justice. Not to report Sabina missing—his distrust of the police and their methods was too deeply ingrained; there was nothing they could do that he couldn't. And not to consult again with Lieutenant William Price. It was probable that Price would not be on duty, and if he'd received any new and important information on Jeffrey Gaunt, he would have sent word.

Quincannon went to the Hall of Justice because that was where the city morgue was located.

Before doing anything else, he had to cement his conviction that Sabina was alive. He said a silent prayer when he stepped into the morgue's dank confines. Had any young women, as yet unidentified, been found and brought in since Friday night? Only one, the morgue attendant told him, the victim of a stabbing on Pacific Avenue. A soiled dove, according to the police report. Quincannon viewed the corpse anyway, just to be sure. And said another silent prayer, this one thankful, when he walked out.

The rest of Sunday night and all of Monday morning he spent checking the guest lists at a dozen hotels large and small—Gaunt was not registered at any of them, nor was any man answering his description—and roaming the Uptown Tenderloin, the Barbary Coast and its fringes, Tar Flat, the waterfront area. He questioned the "gypsy" fortune-teller who called herself Madame Louella, the bunco steerer who went by the moniker of Breezy Ned, the hoodlum named Luther James, the "blind" newsy Slewfoot, and other informants and information sellers with whom he and Sabina had had past dealings. He spoke to Charles Riley, owner of the high-toned House of Chance on Post Street, and the proprietors of other gambling halls from the semi-respectable to the meanest of the Coast's deadfalls. He even paid brief visits to Madame Fifi's Maison of Parisian Delights and Bessie Hall, the "Queen of O'Farrell Street," on the off chance that Gaunt had been one of their customers.

He learned nothing.

No one had seen Gaunt. No one had seen Sabina.

The grim futility of his search had been pointed up in advance by Ezra Bluefield when Quincannon called on him at the Redemption Saloon, his first stop after leaving the Hall of Justice Sunday night. What the ex-miner, ex-Coast denizen had told him, after commiserating over Sabina's disappearance and lamenting his inability to help find her or Gaunt, had not deterred Quincannon at the time. But by noon on Monday there was no gainsaying its bitter truth.

"I hate like the devil to say this, John, my lad," Bluefield said, "but if this bastard Gaunt is in the city, he has made no contact with gamblers, sure-thing men, or others of their ilk."

"You're certain such a meeting couldn't have been kept secret?"

"You know as well as I do there are no secrets in the Coast or the Tenderloin. Any can be bought for as little as the price of a beer." For emphasis Bluefield raised his mug of lager, his favorite tipple; he consumed prodigious quantities day and night. "Lady One-Eye's name is known to several after the shooting of her husband in Grass Valley, but none ever sat at table with her or with Jack O'Diamonds. And none even knew Gaunt's name."

"He must know someone here," Quincannon insisted.

Bluefield drank from his mug, licked foam off his coal-black handlebar mustache. Its waxed, sharp-pointed ends quivered when he said, "Ah, lad, why must he? A man bent on mayhem seldom asks for aid."

"He doesn't if he intends to strike from ambush, shoot down his victim in cold blood, but there is no indication that is what happened to Sabina. If he had something else in mind, he might well seek assistance."

"Something such as what? A kidnapping?"

"I wouldn't put it past him."

"What would he stand to gain by such an act?"

"I don't know. What I do know, what I feel in my bones, is that she is still alive."

Bluefield said nothing. But his thinking was plain: Gaunt may in fact have murdered Sabina in cold blood and disposed of her body in such a fashion that it had yet to be found or might never be found.

Fighting exhaustion—Quincannon had gone home for just a short time, slept hardly at all—he drove to the Western Union office on Market Street. The last two collect wires answering his queries about Gaunt and Lady One-Eye were waiting, but neither contained any useful information.

Onward, then, to Carpenter and Quincannon, Professional Detective Services. The morsel of hope that he might find Sabina there at her desk, safe and with a rational explanation for her absence, died when he found the door locked and the morning's mail on the floor inside. He sifted quickly through the envelopes. No messages and nothing worth opening in the batch.

He tossed the lot onto his desk. The wires from Sheriff Hezekiah Thorpe and the Pinkerton office in New Orleans caught his eye where he'd left them on Sabina's blotter. He sat in her chair, smudged a hand over his face and knuckled his tired eyes, then reread the wires—doing that because he had nothing else to do at the moment.

D. S. Nickerson.

He passed over the name in the Pinkerton wire, then paused and looked at it again. D. S. Nickerson, Gaunt's coconspirator in a land-speculation fraud in New Orleans five years ago. Neither man had been prosecuted. Gaunt had been declared persona non grata by the local constabulary as a result of his suspected involvement in the gambler's murder, at a time when he was already under police scrutiny for the land swindle. Had his partner, Nickerson, also been sent packing from the gulf city? And if so, was it possible he'd come to the Far West to establish a new life?

Quincannon rummaged up the agency's copy of *Langley's City Directory*. He found no listing under the heading of "Real Estate," but when he turned to "Land Agents"—

Donald S. Nickerson, Fifth and Townsend

His first rush of excitement lasted only a few seconds. Don't go jumping to conclusions, he warned himself. Nickerson was not a common name, though neither was it an obscure one; the similarity in both name and initials could be coincidental. As could Donald S. Nickerson's profession. San Francisco was a long way from New Orleans, five years a long time for two former partners to remain in contact.

Still, it was the best and only lead he had. And how could you possibly find a needle in a haystack without grabbing at straws?

The two-story building on the corner of Fifth and Townsend had seen better days. It was not exactly ramshackle, but various parts of its façade were in need of repair and the whole of a fresh coat of whitewash. According to the directory in the vestibule, it housed an attorney, a manufacturer's agent, a publisher of maps, a purveyor of unidentified novelties, and Donald S. Nickerson, Land Agent, office on the second floor.

Quincannon climbed a creaky staircase, went along a gloomy hallway to the door marked with Nickerson's name and profession. Without knocking, he opened it and stepped inside. The office was composed of two rooms, the one he was in and a slightly smaller one visible through an open doorway at the far end. An unoccupied desk and a smattering of other nondescript and inexpensive furniture half filled this one. Photographs of properties, most of which looked to be industrial, were pinned to the walls.

A chair scraped the floor in the other room and a man appeared in the doorway. Fiftyish, stocky, with a moon face topped by strands of ginger-colored hair combed in a checkerboard pattern over an otherwise bald scalp. The smile he wore was hearty and welcoming, and as artificial as the rows of tobacco-stained teeth it revealed. His brown suit was a touch threadbare, his waistcoat and cravat likewise. Not a particularly successful land agent, whether an honest one or not.

"Ah, good afternoon, sir, good afternoon," he said as he came forward. He had no discernible Southern accent. "Donald S. Nickerson, at your service. How may I help you?"

"By answering a few questions."

"Certainly, sir, certainly. Anything and everything you'd care to know. I have several excellent properties for sale, with and without structures, many at bargain prices—"

"I'm not interested in buying property."

"You're not?" Disappointment dimmed Nickerson's toothy smile. "Well. Selling land, then?"

"Not that, either."

The piggish little eyes turned wary. "You wouldn't be here about the, mmm, bank matter, would you?"

"I'm not a collection agent, no."

"No, of course you aren't," Nickerson said, relieved. "A

minor matter, that business, of no consequence. May I ask your name, sir?"

"Quincannon. John Quincannon."

That erased the smile completely. "The, mmm, the detective?"

"You've heard of me then."

"Oh, yes. You've often been prominent in the news. Yes, quite prominent. Splendid reputation. What, mmm, what brings you to see me?"

"Jeffrey Gaunt."

Nickerson's only visible reaction was a twitch at a corner of his mouth. "I don't believe I know the name. Gaunt, did you say? No, I know no one named Gaunt."

"New Orleans, Mr. Nickerson."

"Mmm? What's that? I don't understand."

"You've never done business there?"

"No, sir. No. Never done business there, never been there. Why do you ask?"

"I'm looking for Gaunt. Looking hard for him."

"Are you? Has he, mmm, done something illegal?"

"Committed a crime that will send him to prison for a long time, if not to the hangman." Quincannon added pointedly, fixing the land agent with a basilisk eye, "And anyone who worked in consort with him, too."

The muscle jumped again in Nickerson's cheek. He cleared his throat phlegmily before he said, "But I don't understand, sir. Why have you come to me about this person?"

"He once worked a land swindle in New Orleans with a man named D. S. Nickerson."

"Oh, mmm, I see. The remarkable similarity of name and profession brought you here. A coincidence, I assure you, a remarkably bizarre coincidence."

"Is it?"

"Yes. Certainly. I am an honest man, honest as the day is long. And as I told you I have never been to New Orleans. Never traveled farther east than the state capital, as a matter of fact. No, never."

That was a barefaced lie. Although Nickerson had no discernible Southern accent, neither did he possess the distinctive pronunciation and inflection of a native Californian. Quincannon continued to stare at him, even more fiercely now.

The land agent blinked several times, finally shifted his gaze. He cleared his throat again and said, "I don't wish to be rude, Mr. Quincannon, but I am rather busy and I would appreciate it if you, mmm, proceeded with your inquiries elsewhere."

"No."

". . . I beg your pardon? I don't—"

"I said no. I'll continue my inquiries right here."

"But there is nothing more I can tell you, sir. Not a blessed thing."

Quincannon had run out of patience. He'd dealt with enough nervous, frightened, culpable liars during the course of his career to recognize when he was in the company of another of the breed. D. S. Nickerson of New Orleans and Donald S. Nickerson of San Francisco were one and the same man, and no mistake.

"The devil there isn't," he snapped. "You can and you will

tell me all you know about Jeffrey Gaunt, past and present. You've seen him recently, haven't you?"

"No! No, I—"

Quincannon advanced on him. Nickerson flinched and back-pedaled, but he didn't get far. Quincannon's left hand caught the front of the land agent's coat and shirt and yanked him to a halt. His right filled with his Navy Colt; he thumbed it to cock, and thrust the barrel along Nickerson's upper lip and tight against his left nostril.

"Now talk," he said in a voice like the crack of a whip. "Where is the son of a bitch?"

22

SABINA

The trough had been fashioned of six-foot metal sections welded together, their flanged edges nailed to the floorboards on each side to hold them in place. Some of the rusted nails had worked or broken loose from the rotting wood; Sabina discovered this when she knelt and felt carefully along the edges. The flange on one section had popped up by half an inch or so from the warped board it was attached to. The protrusion was what she had stubbed the toe of her shoe on.

That section was loose on both sides; it rattled and gave slightly when she slid her fingers under the flange and tugged upward. But she couldn't get enough purchase to lift the flange up any higher, and the sharp metal cut painfully into her finger pads.

There was a restrained excitement inside her now, a sense of purpose at last. Find something to pry up the flanges, something thin and strong enough to act as a fulcrum. The scattered pieces of lumber . . . would any of them do? No, they were all too thick.

She went again to the rowboat skeleton. The first thing she did was to send the rowboat crashing to the floor by kicking the fractured leg of the sawhorse holding up its lower end. As she'd hoped, some of the gray bones cracked loose. She felt them until she came upon one that had a split in it. The smaller, splintered piece felt as though it might be what she needed . . . if she could break it free.

Perspiring in the cold dampness, she worked in vain with her fingers and the pipe. Then she thought to try slipping the hollow pipe over the splinter's thin, sharp end. The aperture was just large enough to swallow a couple of inches of wood.

She struggled to get the splinter deeper into the pipe, to gain enough purchase to jerk it up and down, from side to side. Finally it cracked and broke off. She separated it from the pipe, felt along its length. The piece was some eighteen inches long, the broken end less than half an inch thick. Not too thick to wedge under the lip of the flange, she prayed.

It just fit. She wiggled it in as far as it would go, then reinserted the sharp end into the pipe. Now she had an effective pry bar, or she did if the wormy old wood didn't disintegrate from the pressure.

She tore two strips from the hem of her tattered dress, wrapped them around her sore hands, and began laboring. Her strength soon flagged from the exertion; she forced herself to take her time, to rest at intervals. Countless minutes passed before her efforts were rewarded by the screech of another nail pulling free. When it did, the metal rose enough for her to slide the wood farther underneath, thus easing the strain.

A third nail popped out, then a fourth on the opposite side. The section felt wobbly now. Sabina withdrew the wood, took hold of the flange with both hands and jerked upward as hard as she could. The fifth or sixth time she did that, there was another rending metal sound as one or more of the welds fastening this section to the others snapped.

She heaved and twisted frenziedly, raising puffs of the dust and powdery rat droppings that had collected in the hollow. More welds broke apart, another nail came out, and all at once the section parted on both ends, the flange on the opposite side pulled up out of the floorboard. She held the section in one bloodied hand, staggered upright, braced herself, and took a two-handed grip. It took only one more twist to free it completely. She thrust the length of metal from her, sent it clattering to one side.

On her knees again, she peered into the six-foot opening in the floor. She could make out the murky water below, smell its briny odor, feel the chill of the lapping wavelets. How far down? Six feet, eight, more? She couldn't tell. But no matter how far it was, the water couldn't be very deep, not with this part of the building canted downward on pilings.

But could she get out through the gap?

She leaned across it, measuring. As she'd estimated before, it was some eight inches wide, not wide enough even for a woman of her slender frame to squeeze through. The space had to be enlarged a few more inches on one side or the other. She felt the near edge of the floorboard. The wood was wet, rotted, or else she would not have been able to pry up the flange.

More work with the pipe. Chip away at the rotted wood, keep chipping away for as long as it took to widen the opening. It could be done. Freedom, her one and only hope . . . it *had* to be done.

She set to the task.

Bits and pieces of wood flaked off at an agonizingly slow pace. After a while all awareness of time ceased. Her mind was a blank; only dimly did she feel the pain in her cramped joints, her lacerated hands. She became a machine, a human piston, constantly beating away at the one small obstacle between her and escape.

Fatigue and muscle cramps took their toll eventually, forcing another period of rest. She sat back, flexing her hands, her legs. For a moment, then, she closed her eyes. Just for a moment . . . except that exhaustion turned it into minutes, how many she never knew.

The sudden shrill scream of a gull swooping low above the hole in the roof snapped her back to awareness. Her mind, her movements were sluggish at first; she shook herself, mentally as well as physically, until she was able to focus again.

She pushed back onto her knees, felt along the ragged edge of the floorboard. She'd made progress; almost half of it had been chopped through. But not enough yet to attempt to eel her body through the trough opening. The gap had to be widened even more. Lengthened, too.

The fabric around her hands was slick with blood. She peeled off the sodden strips, tore two more from the hem of her dress and rebound her hands. Then she took up the pipe and resumed her labors.

As before, she lost all perception of the passage of time. Gouge with the pipe, rest briefly, measure her progress; gouge with the pipe, rest, measure; gouge, rest, measure . . .

Much of the board was gone now, the floor opening at least ten inches wide. Enough? Not dressed as she was, in the filthy cape and the remains of her evening gown. She struggled out of the clothing, heaped it to one side. Clad only in her shoes and combination undergarment of silk camisole and drawers, she eased herself into a sitting position with her legs thrust through the opening, then pushed forward into it with her elbows braced on either side.

Her hips would not fit through the gap. No matter how much she squirmed, the boards held her in a tight grip.

A frustrated cry formed in her throat; she bit her lip so that the only sound she made was a low moan. She wiggled and pulled herself out and onto the floor, lay panting from the exertion. The next time she made the attempt she would have to succeed. She wouldn't have enough strength left by then to extricate herself from the hole a second time.

Shivers brought on by the cold roused her. The rough wood had torn her undergarment, scraped her skin raw in places. She swept up the cape, encased herself in it. When the shivering subsided, she rewrapped her hands with more strips from the hem of her dress, then set her jaw and once more picked up the pipe.

More lost time while she gouged, rested, measured. And felt herself growing weaker and weaker. Dimly she wondered if she ought to give it up for the time being, crawl back onto the cot in the office, sleep until some of her vigor was renewed . . . no. No. She was not going to get any stronger; lack of food and water would see to that. And as exhausted as she was, if she let herself sleep, God only knew how long she would be unconscious. It was only afternoon now; she might wake up in the middle of the night, and the prospect of another night in the place was intolerable. If she had any chance at all of escaping, it had to be soon, very soon.

She felt along the edge of the board again. Better than half of it had disintegrated. A little more, just a little more . . .

The pipe slipped out of her grasp, fell through the gap into the gurgling water below.

Oh God, now she had no choice. Now she had to make the one last effort.

She said a silent prayer, removed the bloody strips from her hands, shed the cape again. But she had the presence of mind to place it close to the edge, where she could reach it when she lowered herself into the opening. If she succeeded in getting through, she would pull it with her. The bay water was bound to be freezing; without something to cover her near-nakedness, she would die of hypothermia. If she didn't succeed, she wouldn't need the cape—she would die here anyway.

Into the hole then, bracing herself with her elbows as before, the fingers of her right hand clutching the cape. She wiggled lower. The floorboards held her again. She squirmed, twisted—

Let go of me, let go!

—and her hips scraped through. Instinctively she raised

her arms, pulling the cape with her, as the weight of her shoes sent her plunging downward.

The fall was short, no more than six feet, and the water shallow so that her feet jarred through it into soft mud. The icy shock took her breath away. Gasping, she lost her balance, fell sideways into a nest of marsh weeds. Salt water poured into her open mouth, choking her. She coughed it out as she fought upright. The cape had slipped out of her clutch, but she could see it floating next to one of the slimy pilings.

The mud sucked at her shoes; she had difficulty pulling free, staggering ahead to gather the cape and then to where the shoreline slanted upward. The ground was more solid there, matted and thickly grown with weeds and marsh grass. She stumbled upward past the last of the pilings. Just as she emerged from under the building, something caught her ankle and sent her sprawling.

She lay facedown in the grass, laboring to catch her breath. Tremors racked her. But the frigid water had had a revitalizing effect, too, clearing her mind and giving her back some of her strength. She rose up onto her knees. The grass was wet from the fog, she realized then, and the cupped leaves on some of the weeds glistened with moisture. Water, fresh water. She bent her head to the leaves, lapping at the dew like a cat at a bowl of cream. Then she tore up handfuls of grass and sucked on the stems. Her thirst still raged, but the moisture alleviated a little of the terrible burning in her mouth and throat, allowed her to swallow again.

She gained her feet and, dragging the cape, slogged out to where she had a more or less clear view of her surroundings.

The area, overlaid with a thin, windblown fog, was every bit as desolate as she'd imagined. There was another, smaller building besides the one in which she'd been imprisoned, less well built, one wall leaning near collapse. A ghostlike confusion of erections that had something to do with boat storage loomed beyond that. That was all there was to see except for acres of barren marshland and gray, white-flecked water, the outer reaches of both land and bay obscured by mist. The only sounds were the fog warnings and the distant cry of a gull.

The cape was sodden; Sabina twisted some of the water out of it, swirled it around her. Its clamminess increased her trembling. Still, it provided some protection from the wind. Without it, in nothing but her thin, torn undergarment, she would soon freeze.

She slogged to the front of the repair shop, tearing up and sucking more wet grass on the way. There must be some sort of road that led in here . . . Yes, over there—half-hidden parallel ruts, the grass and weeds between them trampled by the passage of the brougham or whatever conveyance Gaunt had used to bring her here.

How far to the nearest habitation? No way of knowing. She hadn't the stamina to trek very far in the open, but there was no choice except to try. There was no shelter here, and once night came . . .

She set off along the ruts. At first her legs were so stiff she felt as though she were moving in place, without progress, as if in a nightmare. But then, gradually, the stiffness eased and she was able to walk without stumbling. Her legs were wobbly but she managed to quicken her pace a bit.

She hadn't gone far when she heard the clattering.

It came from somewhere in the mist ahead of her. She came to a standstill, listening. The noise was faint at first, then progressively louder. A vehicle of some kind, moving rapidly. She knew that for certain when the wheel clatter was joined by the whinny of a horse.

Her first reaction was one of relief, elation, but it lasted only a moment or two. A spiral of fear replaced it. Gaunt! Come back to check on her after all. Who else would be out on this wasteland at this time of day?

The equipage was still unseen, somewhere just beyond a mist-shrouded line of trees. Close now, very close.

Sabina flung herself off the rutted trail, into a patch of high grass prickly with thistles. And lay hugging the ground, trembling again, waiting for Gaunt to pass her by.

23

QUINCANNON

D. S. Nickerson made a strangled-chicken sound, his eyes crossed and bulging as he stared at the gun barrel tickling his nose. His moon face had gone as white as clabbered milk.

"Answer my question, Nickerson, and be quick about it. Where's Gaunt?"

"I . . . I . . . I . . . I . . ."

"Where, damn you!"

"I . . . I . . . don't know . . ."

Quincannon marched him backward into what was evidently his private office, shoved him into a desk chair, and then loomed over him with the Navy now pointed a half inch from his chin. "No more lies, blast you, and no more evasions. My partner has disappeared and Gaunt is surely responsible. I have no qualms about shooting him and none about shooting you or anyone else who aided and abetted him."

Nickerson swallowed audibly, his Adam's apple bobbing

like a cork on a string. "I'm not . . . not l-lying," he stammered. "I'd t-tell you if I knew where he went, but I don't, I s-swear I don't! Please, you have to believe me—!"

"When did you last see him?"

"S-Saturday morning."

"Where?"

"Here, when he returned my equipage."

"What equipage?"

"Brougham. My . . . brougham."

"You gave him the use of it? When?"

"Friday afternoon."

"What did he want it for?"

"He wouldn't say. Wouldn't tell me anything."

"And I suppose you handed it over to him for old time's sake."

"N-no, it wasn't like that." Nickerson swallowed again. He couldn't seem to take his widened eyes off the Navy's barrel, his expression that of a man gawping at a poisonous snake about to strike.

"Paid you for its use?"

"No. I . . . I had to do what he asked. I had no choice."

"He threatened you?"

"Yes. Yes." Now it was Nickerson's head that bobbed up and down. His terrified stammer had abated; words came rushing out of him in a torrent. "He said he'd ruin me . . . kill me if I didn't help him and keep my mouth shut afterward. He meant it, he's . . . I think he must be insane. I was a fool to ever become involved with him. I couldn't believe it when he showed up here, the first time I'd set eyes on him in five years.

I thought I was free of him when I left New Orleans. I . . . I don't know how he found out I came to San Francisco, he wouldn't tell me that, either. . . ."

"Did he say anything about his sister, Lady One-Eye?"

"No. I asked about her . . . news of her arrest in Grass Valley for shooting her husband was in the local papers, your name and your partner's, too . . . but he told me to mind my own business."

"Use of your brougham wasn't all he wanted. What else?"

"One of my . . . my holdings."

"Property holdings? Which one? Where?"

"He had no particular one in mind and he didn't care where it was, just that it be isolated and have an empty building on it."

"And you had such a property."

"An old repair shop for boats in the oyster trade," Nickerson said, "abandoned when the owner died. A white elephant I acquired for a paltry sum at a tax sale two years ago. Not a single prospective buyer since, despite my low asking price—"

"Located where?"

"The South Basin marshes. Gaunt made me drive him down there to look at it inside and out on Friday morning."

"What condition is it in?"

"Good enough, for a derelict building. Gaunt was satisfied with it. He demanded the key to the padlock, then warned me to take the property off the market and keep it off, and to never set foot on it again. I . . . didn't ask him why he wanted it. I didn't want to know."

"No, of course you didn't." But Quincannon knew, and

the thought chilled him to the marrow. An abandoned boat repair shop on the marshland at the south end of the city. Isolated, freezing cold even in the daytime, no doubt rat infested. Dear sweet Jesus! "Exactly where is it located?" he demanded. "You must have a map. Point it out to me."

Nickerson's eyes were still on the Navy. Quincannon lowered the weapon, but kept it on full cock. The land agent pushed himself to his feet, went shakily to a draftsman's cabinet on the wall behind the desk. From one of its deep drawers he found and extracted a map, laid it out on the desk, then backed away to give Quincannon plenty of room to examine it.

There were three marks on the South Basin side of the point, above the outermost jut of land. Quincannon knew the area, an isolated bayfront section east of the Southern Pacific right-of-way; according to the map, the nearest habitation was a sheepskin tannery half a mile or so distant. A squiggly line represented a wagon road that led to the derelict property from the closest thoroughfare, Jamestown Avenue.

"Three marks indicate three structures," Quincannon said. "What are the other two?"

"No, two is all there is. The repair shop and a storage shed. The third mark is for dry-dock and hoist facilities. The pier behind the shop is in unsafe condition—"

"Damn the pier."

The sharpness of the exclamation caused Nickerson to flinch again. He took another unsteady step backward.

"I'll take the key now," Quincannon said.

"Key?"

"Don't be dense. The padlock key."

"I . . . I don't have it."

"Don't have it?"

"Gaunt didn't return it when he returned the brougham on Saturday. When I asked him for it, he said he threw it away so I wouldn't be tempted to go back out there. . . ."

Anger swelled in Quincannon again. He gave vent to a blistering nine-jointed oath of such inventive ferocity not even the likes of a shanghai crimp could have matched it. The outburst caused Nickerson to cringe in terror. He took another unsteady step backward, up against the wall beside the draftsman's cabinet.

In a near-whisper he said, stammering again, "W-what are you g-going to do now?"

"What do you think I'm going to do? Get inside that damned building if I have to batter down the walls to do it."

"You won't find G-Gaunt there. He—"

"I don't expect to find him there. You're sure you have no idea where he went after he left you on Saturday?"

"None. No, none." Nickerson's Adam's apple went a-bobbing again. "What . . . what about me?"

"What about you?"

"You don't intend to . . . to . . ."

"Shoot you? Not if you've been truthful, told me everything you know."

"I have, I s-swear I have."

"Then I'll leave you to stew in your own juices." Quincannon added, glowering malignantly, "But if I find out you lied to me, or if you tell anyone I was here, I'll come back and give you the beating of your life. Yes, and shoot off one of your ears for good measure. Understood?"

"Uh . . . uh . . . uh . . . understood."

Quincannon left the land agent cowering against the wall, hurried out of the building and upstreet to where the rented buggy was parked. It was after three o'clock now. Low-hanging clouds and streamers of fog darkened the afternoon, and a sharp wind off the bay had lowered the temperature by several degrees. Out on the marshes it would be colder still—a frigid night ahead in such an unprotected area.

He climbed up onto the seat, took up the reins and whip-flicked the roan into as fast a trot as traffic would permit.

The drive to South Basin took nearly an hour and seemed twice as long. He couldn't maintain the headlong pace he'd have preferred for fear of exhausting the horse. Stopping en route to acquire such tools as a pry bar and sledgehammer would have wasted even more time; he would have to make do with whatever he found on the abandoned property to gain access to the shop. Sabina must not spend another night in that place.

He refused to think of what her condition might be after three days' incarceration. When he thought at all, it was with a burning hate for Jeffrey Gaunt. Nickerson had been right: the man was insane. Only a maniac would devise and carry out such an evil trick, the torturous destruction of one woman in order to save another.

The land agent's directions were true: Quincannon had no difficulty locating what was left of the old wagon road that led across the marshes to the point. The ruts, potholed in places, choked with weeds and grass, forced him to an even slower pace to avoid breaking an axle. As it was, the buggy jolted and rattled and he had to use the whip, something he disliked doing in normal circumstances, to keep the tired roan from balking. Low-hanging swirls of fog lowered visibility to no more than a hundred yards. Wind gusts carrying faint odors from the tannery chilled his face, twice threatened to tear the buggy's hood loose from its fastenings.

He hunched forward as the remains of the boat-repair business finally appeared ahead, ghost shapes rising out of the mist. Sight of them increased his urgency twofold. God Almighty, what a miserable place! He flicked the whip again to quicken the horse across the remaining distance, drew rein a dozen rods from the entrance to the main building. He set the brake, jumped down, ran to the rust-flecked corrugated iron doors.

The padlock was stout and secure; one hard yank told him that. He beat on one of the door halves with his gloved fist, shouted Sabina's name half a dozen times at the top of his voice. The noise he made shattered the cottony stillness, roused a fluttering group of shorebirds nearby, sent echoes chasing one another across the wasteland. He paused to listen, then pounded on the doors and yelled her name again. And again. And again.

There was no response from within.

Frantic now, Quincannon turned away and ran past the buggy and the blowing roan to the tumbledown shed. There was nothing inside it he could use to break the padlock, nothing at all except planks and fragments of tarpaper from its half-collapsed walls and roof. Outside again, he headed toward where the skeletal remains of hoist and dry-dock facilities jutted up out of nests of tall grass and weeds.

That was when he heard the cry in the mist.

At first he thought it was a gull or some other bird, but when it came again he jerked to a stop. Not a bird, a voice shouting *his* name. Then he saw the figure materialize like an apparition on the wagon ruts thirty yards away, come stumbling toward him.

Sabina!

Emotion overwhelmed him as he ran to meet her. She was both a wonderful and a ghastly sight. Her face scratched and mud flecked, her hair hanging in wet, tangled strands like black seaweed, her hands and arms raw with cuts and blisters, her slender body draped in a filthy, sodden evening cape. And she was in the grip of exhaustion; he reached her just in time to keep her from falling, held her by the arms for a moment, then embraced her as gently as the intensity of his feelings would allow. She clung to him, shivering.

"I heard you shouting," she said in a ragged half whisper. "I was hiding when you went by in the buggy, I couldn't see you under the hood and I thought you were Gaunt. How did you know to come here . . . ?"

This was not the time for explanations, either his, or hers

of how she'd escaped the padlocked repair shop. "Not now. You need to get out of those wet clothes, then away from here and into a doctor's care."

"I'm . . . not badly hurt."

"The risk of pneumonia, my dear."

Quincannon lifted her into his arms, carried her to the buggy, placed her on the seat. She protested mildly when he took off the cape, the reason being that she wore nothing else except a wet, torn, muddy undergarment, but this was not the time for modesty, either. Swiftly he shed his greatcoat and slipped it around her. "Button yourself in after you've removed the undergarment," he said. "I'll wait with my back turned until you're ready."

It didn't take her long. When she called him back, he climbed up beside her and removed his hat, placed it on her head; as large as it was, it came down to eye level, covering most of her wet hair and serving as further protection from the cold. He would have given her his gloves, too, but she already had her injured hands thrust deep into the coat pockets.

He took hold of the reins. Before he started the horse moving, he slipped his other arm around her shoulders and drew her against him. "To help keep you warm," he said.

"Yes, my dear, I know."

Despite the dire circumstances, her words deepened the tenderness he felt for her. He had addressed her as "my dear" on countless occasions, casually and not so casually; this was the first time she had ever used that term of endearment in return.

24

QUINCANNON

The nearest physician he knew of was one he'd had dealings with before—Dr. Emil Jorgensen, whose home and practice were on Third Street. The doctor provided regular treatments for the chronic gout suffered by Mr. Boggs, head of the San Francisco branch of the Secret Service and Quincannon's former boss, and Quincannon had once had occasion to call on him for treatment of a minor gunshot wound. Jorgensen was competent, trustworthy, and discreet.

On the interminable buggy ride, there was little conversation until after they had crossed out of the marshland. Sabina pressed close, her hands thrust into the pockets of the greatcoat; its woolen warmth and Quincannon's body heat ended her shivering except for a few random tremors. He was chilled himself, dressed as he was now in only his suit, vest, and gloves, but his own discomfort was of no consequence to him. His concern was entirely for Sabina's welfare. He urged her to close her eyes and try to sleep, but the lurching and rattling of the carriage rendered that impossible.

Once they were back on city streets, she roused somewhat and asked him again how he'd known where she was. He told her. Then he asked the question that was uppermost in his mind.

"Did Gaunt harm you in any way?"

"No. Not in the sense you mean. An arm around my neck and a cloth soaked in ether over my nose and mouth. He was gone when I woke up in that . . . place."

"And he didn't come back at any time?"

"No. Simply left me there without food or water."

To die of starvation or, far worse, the merciless assault of hungry rats. Damn Gaunt's black soul to hell!

"How did you manage to escape?"

"By luck and force of will." She briefly summarized the method she'd used; it was plain that she had no desire to relive the experience in detail. "If I had had an inkling that you'd be able to find me, I wouldn't have been quite so desperate to get out."

"But you didn't. You couldn't have. You did what you had to do to save yourself."

It must have been after six o'clock when they finally reached Dr. Jorgensen's. Fortunately he kept late office hours and there were no patients present when Quincannon helped Sabina inside. The doctor's wife also served as his nurse; she took immediate charge of Sabina, ushering her into the surgery to cleanse her and provide hot liquids and garments to cover her nakedness, while Quincannon tersely explained to Jorgensen what had happened, making no mention of Jeffrey Gaunt's name or the circumstances that had led to Sabina's weakened and wounded condition. No questions were forthcoming; the doctor's only interest, as always, was in fulfilling his Hippocratic oath and otherwise minding his own business. When Sabina was ready to be examined and her injuries treated, he hurried out without a word.

Quincannon waited, pacing and fidgeting in the anteroom. Every time his thoughts touched on Jeffrey Gaunt, a wild fury took hold of him. But it was an impotent fury, here and now, and served no purpose except to raise his blood pressure to the danger level. The time for retribution would come. Not soon enough to suit him, but not far off, either.

Mrs. Jorgensen appeared with a steaming mug of coffee for him. She wouldn't say anything about Sabina's condition; that was the doctor's purview when he finished his ministrations.

Half an hour crawled away. And another fifteen minutes before Jorgensen appeared. His thin, ascetic face was as expressionless as always, but there was reassurance in his voice when he spoke. "Mrs. Carpenter is as well as can be expected under the circumstances. Hypothermia, three days without water or nourishment, numerous lacerations and abrasions . . . most women would be prostrated by such an ordeal."

"She will be all right?"

"Barring the onset of pneumonia, yes, and I could detect no pulmonary edema—fluid in the lungs. Complete bed rest is indicated. I recommend she remain here for two or three days, where my wife and I can keep a close eye on her. We have the facilities, as you know."

"Whatever you say, Doctor. I'd like to see her before I leave."

"I've given her a sleeping draught. But yes, briefly, if she is still awake."

Sabina was in the Jorgensens' two-bed ward at the rear of the house. Both her hands had been bandaged, iodoform dabbed on a facial cut, and her hair rubbed dry and covered with a woolen cap. She appeared small and pale and very young—an image that brought a lump to Quincannon's throat.

"Don't look at me like that," she said. "I know I look a fright, but I'm not at death's door yet."

He managed a small smile. "Of course you're not. You'll be fine after a few days' rest."

"John . . . what are you going to do about Gaunt?"

"Find him, as fast I can."

"He's not in the city. He had no reason to stay. I think he went back to Grass Valley to be near Lady One-Eye."

"Yes. So do I."

"So you intend to go up there after him. And then what?"

Quincannon said carefully, "That depends on him."

"You mustn't shoot him down in cold blood. I don't want that kind of vengeance." Her eyelids fluttered, closed, as the sleeping draught took effect. "Promise me, John."

He didn't have to promise her, for in the next few seconds, consciousness left her. Just as well, because the promise would have been one he was not at all sure he'd be able to keep.

Before leaving, Quincannon told Dr. Jorgensen that a pressing business matter would prevent him from returning for at least two days. There was no need to impart this information to Sabina when she awakened, he said; she would know where he'd gone and why. Payment for the physician's services was not mentioned. Jorgensen's fees were reasonable, and he knew that Quincannon, like Mr. Boggs, was scrupulous in honoring his debts.

He drove to the United Carriage Company's stables on Eighth Street, where he relinquished the rented horse and buggy. Without objection, he paid an extra fee for what the dour hostler referred to, after a brief examination, as "undue wear and tear" on both animal and equipage. Then he hired a cab to take him to his flat.

Although he had no appetite, he hadn't eaten a bite in twenty-four hours—a sandwich quickly consumed during his Sunday-night rounds. And Sabina's weakened condition was a sharp reminder of the need for sustenance. He kept little enough in the way of provisions at the flat, taking most of his meals in restaurants and Hoolihan's Saloon, but he found a wedge of cheese and half a loaf of stale bread and forced down another sandwich.

Rest was another necessary commodity, the more so for what lay ahead of him on the morrow. He packed a few things into his traveling valise, among them extra cartridges for his Navy Colt, then crawled into bed. As weary as he was, sleep came easily enough—but not before he set his reliable internal clock for five A.M.

25

QUINCANNON

With Sabina for company, time had passed swiftly enough on his previous trips on the eastbound Southern Pacific train into the Sierras. This one dragged interminably. He couldn't seem to sit still, got up from his seat every few minutes to pace through the cars.

When they arrived at last at Colfax, his patience was further tested by a thirty-minute wait for the next Nevada County Narrow Gauge train. By the time that slow conveyance, with its numerous passenger stops, traversed the three miles from Nevada City to the Grass Valley station, it was after three o'clock and his patience was gone, his temper short, and his simmering anger near the boiling point.

Waves of sticky heat assailed him as he made his way up East Main to the city jail. Back and forth the past week from sweatbox to summer chill to sweatbox—bah! Now all he needed was for Sheriff Hezekiah Thorpe to be away from his office.

But he was spared that, at least. Thorpe was present, seated at his desk under a sluggish fan, sweat glistening on his seamed and side-whiskered face. He blinked his surprise at seeing Quincannon come marching in.

"What in tucket brings you back here?"

"Jeffrey Gaunt."

"Gaunt? Didn't you get my wire?"

"That he'd left Grass Valley for parts unknown, yes."

"Not that one," Thorpe said, "the one I sent yesterday afternoon."

"No, I didn't." It must have come in after he'd left the agency offices to pay his call on D. S. Nickerson. "What did it say?"

"That Gaunt's back. Seems he went down to Sacramento to arrange with a lawyer to represent his sister at the trial."

The devil he did! "He tell you that himself?"

"When he came in to visit her. I sent the wire right afterward."

"Where can I find him?"

Thorpe, a shrewd old bird, sensed the tension and anger in Quincannon. "What do you want with him? You got some kind of bone to pick?"

Quincannon was not about to confide his purpose, not yet. The sheriff would either try to talk him out of it, or demand to join forces with him, and Thorpe had no more legal standing than he did, Sabina's abduction having taken place in San Francisco. No matter how it played out, this was between Quincannon and Gaunt and nobody else.

He said shortly, "Personal business. Where is he lodged? The Holbrooke?"

"No. Same place he's been staying ever since Amos McFinn evicted him. Lily Dumont's cottage."

"What? You mean with her?"

"No. She packed up and made herself scarce right after you and Mrs. Carpenter left," Thorpe said. "Afraid of what Glen Bonnifield might do to her, I reckon. He was keeping her, all right. And damn mad when he recovered. Went and talked to Gaunt, or vice versa—I never did get the straight of that—and they worked up an arrangement."

"You wouldn't happen to know if Gaunt is at the cottage now?"

"Nope. He came in to see Lady One-Eye earlier, but where he went after that I couldn't tell you." The sheriff paused; his gaze held steely glints. "This personal business you have with Gaunt. Must be pretty important to bring you all the way up here now, with the trial only a few days off."

"It is. Very important."

"Won't jeopardize the case against Lady One-Eye, will it?"

"On the contrary," Quincannon said. "One way or another, it'll ensure that she's convicted."

"One way or another? You want to elaborate on that?"

"Not now, Sheriff. Later, after I have my talk with Gaunt."

"You listen here now, I don't want any more trouble in my town—"

But Quincannon wasn't listening. He was already on his way out.

Gaunt was not at Lily Dumont's cottage.

Quincannon rattled his knuckles loudly on the door several

times before subsiding. What now? It was too blasted hot to chase around hunting his quarry; Gaunt could be anywhere in Grass Valley, or in Nevada City at Bonnifield's Ace High Saloon. On impulse Quincannon tried the door latch. Locked, naturally. He could pick the lock, or the one on the rear door as he'd done that night the previous week, and wait inside to catch Gaunt by surprise. But that was a mug's game, the disadvantage outweighing the advantage. Illegal trespass would not mitigate in his favor with Sheriff Thorpe no matter how the confrontation with Gaunt played out.

A pine tree grew close to the far end of the porch, and a tall oleander shrub grew around the corner in front; together they created a patch of deep shade. And drawn up against the railing there was a cane-bottom chair. As good a place as any to do his waiting, he decided. He positioned the chair so that it would be hidden from the street and most of the front walk. Gaunt wouldn't see him until he reached the porch steps and started up.

It was a fairly long wait. Now that he was here, now that the meeting with Gaunt was imminent, enough of Quincannon's patience returned to make the waiting tolerable. The shade helped, too, holding off the sweltering heat so that his face and hands remained more or less dry. He sat quietly, his coat thrown open, now and then fingering the handle of the Navy.

His thoughts, when he thought at all, were of Sabina. In his mind's eye he could see her as she came stumbling wraithlike out of the fog; and later, as she lay small and pitiable in Dr. Jorgensen's ward bed. He could feel, too, despite the heat here, the trembling of her wet and chilled body as he carried her to the buggy and when she pressed against him during the long, jouncing ride into the city. The visual and sensory memories added fuel to the hate that bubbled inside him.

Now and then a vehicle rattled by on the street, and some-where in the neighborhood a dog set up a desultory barking, and once he heard the sound of voices as an unseen man and a woman strolled past. Otherwise, the distant, steady pound of ore-crushing stamps at the Empire Mine was the only break in the afternoon stillness.

More than an hour passed. He had just looked at and put away his stem-winder for the third time when he heard foot-falls on the walkway. He sat forward, tensing. It was Gaunt—alone, dressed as always in black despite the temperature.

Quincannon waited until he mounted the last of the steps before gaining his feet and saying, "It's about time, Gaunt."

Gaunt was too self-controlled, too coldly emotionless, to do anything but stop and turn his head. His expression betrayed neither surprise nor alarm, nor even wariness. It was almost as if he'd expected Quincannon. As he surely had, though not this soon.

"Well, the renowned detective," he said in his slow drawl. "How long have you been here?"

Quincannon had himself under tight rein as well—for the moment. "Long enough."

"Why? You must know that the trial isn't until next week."

"The trial isn't what brought me."

"No? Then what did?"

"You know the answer to that."

"I'm afraid not. Suppose you enlighten me."

"Sabina Carpenter."

"Your erstwhile partner. What about her?"

"Her sudden disappearance."

"Oh? Disappeared, you say?"

"Last Friday night in San Francisco."

"That's too bad. How did it happen?"

"She was kidnapped," Quincannon said. Rage was close to the surface now; his voice was thick with it.

"What makes you think that?"

"I don't think it, I know it." He took two steps forward, so that only a few paces separated them. "Kidnapped, locked in an abandoned building without food or water, and left there to die."

Nothing changed in Gaunt's demeanor. One arm hung at his side, the other was drawn up at his middle so that the fingers just touched the flap of his coat. Armed? A hideout weapon within easy reach? Quincannon hoped so, hoped for a sudden draw. He was not sure yet what he would do. Draw himself and fire first, mayhap. Or swing the Navy like a club. Or take the hideout away from him and make him eat it.

"How do you know this?" Gaunt's voice was still cold, without inflection.

"She didn't die, Gaunt. She escaped and I found her. Yesterday afternoon."

"How did she escape? How did you find her?"

"Ingenuity on her part, detective work on mine."

"Are you accusing me of abducting the woman? Is that why you're here?"

"Yes, to both questions."

245

Gaunt's upper lip curled. "The accusation is false and slanderous besides. I was in Sacramento on Friday, consulting with an attorney named Barstow. He'll swear to that if need be."

"A shyster paid to lie."

"Another slanderous statement."

"I can prove you kidnapped her."

"How? Did she see her abductor?"

"He spoke to her and she recognized his voice. Yours."

"But she didn't see the man, did she? And voice recognition is unreliable, the more so at night."

"How would you know she was abducted at night unless you abducted her?"

"I assumed it."

Enough of this cat and mouse. Quincannon said in a flat, hard voice, "The building where you took her and left her to die is an abandoned boat repair shop on the South Basin marsh—property owned by your former land-swindle partner, D. S. Nickerson. He'll testify in court that you coerced him into acting as your accomplice."

Gaunt's mouth thinned to a straight white line, like a knife slash before it begins to bleed. "Damn you, Quincannon. And damn Mrs. Carpenter, too."

"No, damn *you*, you sadistic son of a bitch."

Long, tense seconds passed before Gaunt said, "What do you intend to do? Kill me?"

"If you give me cause."

"And if I don't? Put me under arrest?"

"My license from the state of California gives me that

authority. You'll occupy a cell next to your sister's until the San Francisco police can arrange for extradition."

Some of the ice in Gaunt's eyes thawed. There was an edgy, poised look to him now. His right hand still rested on the front of his waistcoat, the tips of his fingers just touching the lapel of his black frock coat. Quincannon immediately swept the tail of his coat aside with his left hand to expose the holstered Navy, gripped its handle with his right—movements so swift that Gaunt had no time to react.

"Go ahead and draw your hideout weapon," he said. "I'd like nothing better than to shoot you dead where you stand."

The clash of wills continued a few seconds longer, neither man moving, their gazes locked. Then Quincannon said, "Well, Gaunt? Will you come along peaceably or—"

Gaunt's nerve broke. The compulsive protector, the black-hearted avenger, the man supposedly fashioned of ice and iron spun on his heel, leaped down off the porch, and ran.

Quincannon drew the Navy and gave chase, shouting, "Stop, blast you, I'll shoot if you don't!"

The fugitive paid no heed to the warning. He staggered out through the open gate, onto empty, heat-blistered Pleasant Street. There was a gun in his hand now, too, a small pistol, and he skidded to a halt long enough to turn and fire. Quincannon dodged, but the shot was wild, the bullet clipping off an elm branch twenty feet away.

Gaunt commenced running again, plunging headlong downhill toward town. Panic made him fleet of foot, fleet enough to outrace his pursuer to a more populated area and

thus endanger innocent citizens. Quincannon couldn't let that
happen. He slowed, drew a long bead between the fleeing
scoundrel's shoulder blades. But he had never in his life shot
a man in the back, and he couldn't bring himself to do so now.
He lowered his aim, steadied the Navy again, and fired.

His marksmanship was accurate as always. The bullet took
Gaunt just behind the right knee, sent him yelling and tumbling onto the cobblestones. He rolled over twice before
sliding to a stop in a supine sprawl. The pistol was still clutched
in his hand, but he was no longer trying to use it; pain had him
in too tight a grip. Quincannon ran up and kicked the weapon
out of his grasp, stepped over to retrieve it, then stepped back
and stood over him with the Navy pointed downward at the
deep cleft in his chin.

Gaunt stared up at him, grimacing, clutching at his
wounded leg. It had been a clean shot, the slug likely shatter-
ing bone but not piercing an artery; there was little enough
blood. His panic had ebbed swiftly under the lash of agony,
and the man of ice and iron briefly reemerged.

"Go ahead, put a bullet between my eyes and have done
with it. You want to, I can see it in your face."

Quincannon did want to—a measure of his hate for this
soulless excuse for a human being. But he had never killed a
man in cold blood and he was not about to start now, in broad
daylight, with a handful of citizens aroused by the gunfire beginning to congregate. Nor, for that matter, would he have if
the two of them had been alone together on a mountaintop or
the desolate marshland at Candlestick Point. Nothing, he knew

now, not even what had been done to Sabina, could ever make a murderer out of John Frederick Quincannon.

"No," he said, and holstered the Navy, and then caught hold of Gaunt's coat collar and dragged his unpleasant carcass off Pleasant Street.

26

SABINA

When John came to see her late Wednesday afternoon, Sabina was feeling much better. Dr. Jorgensen and his wife had kept her swaddled in blankets and pumped full of medicine that resulted in long hours of healing sleep, and when she was awake, fed her large portions of hot soup, hot tea with honey, and sugared oatmeal (which she had never liked but dutifully ate). The doctor, after his most recent examination, announced that the threat of pneumonia seemed to have passed. If her breathing and her temperature were both normal tomorrow, he said, she would be able to go home.

But it would be another few days before she'd be able to return to her professional duties. The lacerations on her hands and the cut on her cheek needed more time to heal. She didn't ask him if she would be fit to travel next week; she would make the trip to Grass Valley to testify at Lady One-Eye's trial no matter how she felt. Nothing would prevent it now that she had survived Jeffrey Gaunt's vicious attempt to silence her.

Memories of those three terrible days of entrapment would plague her for a long time after her wounds were healed. Her first night here she'd had a nightmare in which a horde of rats pursued her through the murky confines of the building, a dream so vivid and terrifying that she'd awakened from it drenched and shaken. There would be others in the future, she knew, as there had been a succession of nightmares after Stephen was killed. But they would not continue indefinitely, any more than had the ones of Stephen calling her name as he lay mortally wounded. Knowledge that justice had been meted out to Gaunt, as it had been meted out to the bandit who'd shot Stephen, would eventually drive them away.

But it must be the right kind of justice. And it was. John's arrival and account of the confrontation with Gaunt at Lily Dumont's cottage cheered her all the more.

"I must say I'm relieved," she said. "I was afraid that once you found him, you might be angry enough to do something rash."

"Shoot him down like the cur he is?" John shifted in the chair he'd drawn up next to the bed, fluffed his thickening beard. "It occurred to me more than once the past few days to do just that."

"But you didn't act on the impulse, even when he panicked and fled. That is what matters."

"Well, you told me before I left that you had no desire for blood vengeance."

"Did you restrain yourself only on my behalf, or on yours as well?"

"Both. I discovered I'm not as prone to violence as I thought I might be when I confronted him."

"I'm glad. If you had killed Gaunt without provocation—"

"I would have been no better than him. Yes, I know."

"Justice is better served if he suffers the same fate he sought to spare his sister."

"Agreed. Prison is the proper place for criminals whose bags of tricks have been emptied." John fluffed at his whiskers again. "I stopped at the Hall of Justice before coming here and filed a formal complaint against Gaunt for kidnapping and attempted murder. There'll be papers for you to sign before extradition can be arranged."

"As soon as I'm able," Sabina said.

"Which shouldn't be long, judging from how well you look."

"I look a fright and you know it."

"Nonsense. After what you've been through, you look remarkably healthy. Dr. Jorgensen tells me you have the constitution of a horse."

She laughed. "A horse! He did not."

"Well, no, not quite," John admitted. "His exact words were 'Mrs. Carpenter has a strong constitution.' He also said I should be able to take you home tomorrow."

"Yes, he told me the same— Oh!"

"What's the matter?" he said, alarmed. "You're not in pain?"

"No, I just remembered Adam and Eve, my cats. They haven't been fed since last Friday, they'll be starving."

"Oh, but they have been fed more recently than that. I filled their bowls Sunday evening."

"You did?"

"When I couldn't find you anywhere, I suspected you'd run afoul of Gaunt . . . though I never stopped believing you were still alive . . ."

"John, did you pick the lock on the door to my flat?"

He confessed that he had. "An act of desperation—the slim hope of finding a clue to what happened to you."

"The first time you'd ever been inside. I suppose you rummaged through all my things?"

"Of course not," he said indignantly. "Only a cursory examination, and nothing of a personal nature. You don't mind, do you?"

"Since you fed Adam and Eve, no, not at all."

"Under normal circumstances I would never have invaded your private space uninvited—"

"I know you wouldn't." She smiled to reassure him, then on impulse reached out to place her bandaged hand on his. "John . . . thank you."

"For feeding the cats? They were yowling—"

"No, not for that. For all you did to rescue me."

"I didn't rescue you, you rescued yourself."

"From Gaunt's prison, yes, but I might have died anyway on the marshes if you hadn't come when you did. Collapsed and frozen to death before I could walk out—I was at the end of my tether. Your frantic search saved my life."

He said in a softened voice, "There isn't anything I wouldn't do for you, my dear, to keep you safe."

Sabina squeezed his hand, paying no heed to the twinges caused by the pressure. *Nor I for you, my dear,* she thought.